D1051913

BIG BLONDES

The New Press International Fiction Series

BIG BLONDES

Jean Echenoz

Translated from the French by Mark Polizzotti

THE NEW PRESS NEW YORK

© 1995 by Les Editions de Minuit.
English translation © 1997 by Mark Polizzotti.

All rights reserved. No part of this
book may be reproduced, in any form, without
written permission from the publisher.

LIBRARY OF CONGRESS CATALOGING-IN-PUBLICATION DATA

Echenoz, Jean
   [Grandes blondes. English]
   Big blondes / Jean Echenoz; translated from the French
by Mark Polizzotti.
      p.   cm.
   ISBN 1-56584-340-1 (hardcover)
   I. Polizzotti, Mark. II. Title.
PQ2665.C5G7313   1997
843'.914—dc21   96-37226
                   CIP

Originally published in France as *Les Grandes Blondes*
by Les Editions de Minuit, Paris
Published in the United States by The New Press, New York
Distributed by W.W. Norton & Company, Inc., New York

The New Press was established in 1990 as a not-for-profit alternative
to the large, commercial publishing houses currently dominating the book
publishing industry. The New Press operates in the public interest
rather than for private gain, and is committed to publishing, in innovative
ways, works of educational, cultural, and community value that might
not normally be commercially viable.

BOOK DESIGN by Smyth and Whiteside of BAD
PRODUCTION MANAGEMENT by Kim Waymer
PRINTED in the United States of America
9 8 7 6 5 4 3 2 1

BIG BLONDES

C H A P T E R 1

YOU ARE PAUL SALVADOR and you're looking for someone. Winter is coming to an end. But you don't want to do the looking by yourself, you don't have much time, and so you contact Jouve.

You could, as usual, arrange to see him on a bench, in a bar, or in the office—yours or his. For a change of pace, you suggest he meet you at the municipal swimming pool at Porte des Lilas. Jouve is glad to oblige.

On the day in question, you are there at the appointed hour, at the appointed place. But the Paul Salvador you are does not usually show up early for his meetings.

Arriving particularly early that day, Salvador first walked around the large black and white building containing five thousand hectoliters of water. Then, following the slight incline of Boulevard Mortier, he passed in front of the gray constructions that bordered the southern face of the pool building and contained five hundred employees of the French counterintelligence services. Salvador took a stroll around that, too, until, not far in the distance, the bells of Notre-Dame des Otages rang the hour.

He and Jouve met in the pool cafeteria, above the grand-stands that hung over the lanes, beneath the wide, transparent sun roof. The only people in that area wearing business suits (light gray for Salvador, navy blue for Jouve), they watched the bathers flail about at their feet, observing the women more closely than the men, each establishing a private mental typology of their swimwear: the one- or two-piece kind, bikinis or thongs, models with pleats, smocks, ribbons, even flounces. They hadn't yet begun speaking. They waited for their Perrier and lemons.

At the time, Salvador was working for a company that produced TV shows, in charge of entertainment programs and news magazines—entertainment programs and news magazines that Jouve watched every evening with his wife. Salvador, a tall, thin individual of about forty, didn't have a wife. His long pale fingers played with each other constantly, whereas Jouve's hands, more carpenter- or butcher-like, ignored each other, carefully avoided contact, each one ensconced most of the time in one of Jouve's pockets.

Heavy-set, ten years older than Salvador and four inches shorter, Jouve prudently sipped the contents of his glass: the carbonated water and lemon blended with the chlorinated air of the natatorium to gently cleanse his nostrils. "So," he finally said, "who is it this time?" He shook his head when Salvador uttered a woman's name. "Mm, no, I don't think so," he said. "I don't believe I've heard of her."

"Take a look anyway," said Salvador, handing him a ream of press clippings and photos depicting the same young woman, always on the point of departure, with captions mentioning the name Gloria Stella.

Two kinds of photos. On the four-color ones, cut from the glossy pages of weekly magazines, one could see her leaving the stage, or bursting from a Jaguar or a jacuzzi. On the other, slightly more recent ones, in poorly screened black-

and-white garnered from the Society pages of the daily press, you could see her exiting a police station, leaving a lawyer's office, or walking down the steps of a courthouse. If the first batch of photos, perfectly lit, abounded in dazzling smiles and triumphant looks, the second was filled with averted eyes behind dark glasses and closed lips, flattened out by the flashbulbs and hastily centered. "Hang on," said Jouve, "wait a moment."

While waiting, Salvador excused himself. On the door to the toilet stalls, amid various propositions, an exasperated felt pen had inscribed NEITHER LORD NOR SWIMMING MASTER! "I've got it," said Jouve when Salvador retook his seat in the cafeteria. "Now I recognize her. I remember that story. Whatever happened to that girl?"

"No idea," said Salvador. "Vanished four years ago. I'd like you to handle this for me. It shouldn't be too complicated, should it?"

"Shouldn't be," said Jouve. "We'll have to see."

Soon afterward they headed out on foot toward the city's outer boulevards. "Right," Jouve said. "I'll start a file. It would be good if you could write down for me everything you know about her."

"Of course," said Salvador, pulling another paper from his pocket. "I drew this up for you. I've put down everything I could find on this sheet."

"Nice-looking girl, in any case," Jouve pronounced as he leafed through the photos. "Can I keep them?"

"By all means," said Salvador.

With Jouve, Salvador walked once more past the counterintelligence headquarters, of which only the upper floors were visible behind a protective wall bristling with barbed wire and fixed cameras aimed at the sidewalk. At wide intervals, enameled signs bolted to the wall discouraged people from photographing or filming the area, which enjoyed military classification and bore witness to successive styles of administrative architecture from 1860 to 1960. A tall, skinny metal tower supported a number of antennae directed toward the four corners of the earth, and the only means of ingress was a heavy gateway mounted on rails, through which French vehicles containing vague individuals entered and exited nervously. Two uniformed sentries guarded this gateway, with similarly deterrent expressions and somber appearances, their eyes masked by mirrored shades.

"To tell the truth," Salvador said, "this might not be too easy. We looked around a bit ourselves, but came up with nothing. It's as if she hasn't been in touch with anyone in, as I said, almost four years."

"We'll see," said Jouve. "I'll get somebody on it for you right away. But who?" He wondered. "There's Boccara, who wouldn't be bad; I'll see if he's free. Or else Kastner, maybe. Yeah, better Kastner. Nice guy, and he could handle it just fine. First off, is that the right identity?"

"Excuse me?" said Salvador. "What identity?"

"That, her name," said Jouve, putting his finger on Gloria Stella. "Sounds kind of like a fishing boat, don't you think?"

"Oh, right," said Salvador. "Oh, no, no of course not. But you'll see, I put all that down on the sheet."

CHAPTER 2

LATE IN THE AFTERNOON, Jean-Claude Kastner reached the small industrial zone that gave some preliminary idea of Saint-Brieuc. He parked his car in the lot of a pet food factory, then searched in the glove compartment for an opaque plastic pouch, fastened with Velcro, which he set on his knees without opening right away. First he pressed his eyes, with just the tips of his fingers, but hard, to rid them of the 250 miles of highway.

The pouch contained the documents Salvador had given Jouve the day before yesterday, along with Michelin map number 58, detailing Brittany between Lamballe and Brest. In a fold of the peninsula was slipped a handwritten list of port towns swarming up and down the coast, as well as others further inland, from here to Saint-Pol-de-Léon. According to the first cross-checks that Jouve had done, it was there that the woman might be living—a tall, beautiful intimidating blonde woman photographed in various angles and various climates. Tracing his route for the next few days, Jean-Claude Kastner joined together in red pencil, directly on the road map, the townlets that he would have to visit. Once the latter had been connected by a broken line, as in certain magazine games, the route formed no discernible shape, and Kastner found this vaguely disappointing.

Having refolded these materials into their sheath, he started up and got back on the highway, continuing on to Saint-Brieuc. With his car parked in the center of town near the covered market, Kastner dined on a deluxe couscous at one of the Maghreb restaurants that compete with each other near the old station; then he found a room in an unrated hotel opposite the new one. Gloomily lit by a single overhead bulb, the room was a windowless cube with no television or refrigerator, and no toiletries in the bathroom, since there was no bathroom: in a corner they had simply grafted an elementary shower under a tarnished, foldable plastic device, fragile and leaking. Kastner fell asleep fairly quickly.

He woke up just as quickly two hours later, tossed several times in his bed without managing to fall back asleep, turned on the overhead light, then tried to get back into a sci-fi novel whose ins eluded him even more than its outs. The room was too hot, then too cold, and Kastner alternately shivered and perspired, unable to keep his mind on what he was reading. Taking up his road map again, he reworked the itinerary established in the parking lot: it didn't change very much, but this time the resulting drawing vaguely suggested a sea horse lying on its side. In desperation, he ended up swallowing a sleeping pill, dozing off after twenty minutes.

Incoherent dreams passed through him, concluded by a familiar nightmare. The classic vertigo dream: Kastner clings with all his might to the top of a vertical mass of disjointed girders and rusty crossbars hanging over an abyss. It's a precarious scaffolding with peeling paint, which a strong wind is threatening to knock down. Kastner doesn't dare look at the void below him; he feels his energy flagging and his strength deserting him, knowing full well that he is about to let go. The situation is already very distressing, and normally the dream ends there; it's there that his terror generally wakes him. But not this time. This time Kastner loses his grip and falls, falls into the endless void. He wakes up, drenched, just before hitting the ground.

Ordered for seven o'clock, his breakfast consisted of watery, mass-produced coffee, orangeade, and pastry. Kastner didn't have the stomach to finish it. The sleeping pill had left his mouth dry, cut his strength just like in his dream, along with most of his appetite. He was achy, feverish; his fingers trembled a bit. He proceeded to do a few half-hearted deep kneebends, after which his sweat gave off a chemical odor that persisted after a careful shower, persevering even through the eau de toilette. Then he put on the same clothes as the day before: brown polyester suit over a wine-colored polyester polo shirt. In this way, Kastner was dressed like some salesmen or door-to-door canvassers—professions that he had more or less held in the past, as well as several others that enjoyed a similar level of prestige in the social scale of employment.

All day long, at the wheel of his car, the Michelin road map folded out on the right front seat, Kastner followed the prescribed route. Stopping in each little town, he showed his photos to bartenders, service station managers, tripe butchers, or bakers not yet done in by the large supermarkets. He convinced himself he was being discreet. Kastner said that the woman in the photos was his sister, or sometimes his sister-in-law. Once he got up the nerve to pretend she was his wife, but it bothered him, upset him, and he didn't risk it again. In any case, the small shopkeepers shook their heads and pouted negatively, and so

Kastner also canvassed the large supermarkets. But in vain all that day, and all the next.

On the third day it rained, and Kastner got lost. In fact, it rained without really raining; minuscule droplets dotted the windshield—not heavy enough to make it worth using the wipers, not light enough to do without them. The blade smeared the glass instead of washing it. No doubt because of that, while trying to get to a village named Launay-Mal-Nommé, he missed a junction on Route D789, somewhere between Kerpalud and Kervodin, only to find himself smack in the middle of a cluster of anonymous gray houses. He parked on a platform in front of a massive church, with a monument to the dead to the left and a small marine cemetery to the right, which was scarcely more lively: nothing to inspire any joy in the man sitting in his car. He tried to decipher his road map, which by now was more like a rebus. Then he vaguely sought out his name on the monument to the dead, but as usual it was a total loss: only patronyms of local vintage were listed there, which did not include the Kastners.

His glance drifted toward the church, behind which an elderly man no sooner emerged than disappeared; then two minutes later a woman skirted the church door. Kastner, despite all the wrong-way streets in his life, had never liked asking directions of anyone, but this time the ambient dampness, loneliness, and silence led him to lower his window and, as the woman was passing nearby, apologize for bothering her:

"Excuse me," he said, "but I think I've lost my way. I'm looking for an intersection. You wouldn't know anything about an intersection around here, would you?"

The woman was young, slightly stooped: little flat shoes, dull mid-length hair that for lack of better word one would call chestnut brown, large eyeglasses on a small aquiline nose—the whole thing covered in violent makeup and wrapped in a sweatsuit whose halves didn't match. Closed, perhaps fearful expression, nothing attractive, didn't seem mean. She stopped without immediately coming closer, her body leaning to one side under the weight of a bag of groceries. "An intersection," Kastner repeated, "a crossroads."

She appeared at first glance to have no particular ideas on the subject, then not to have very many ideas at all. Doesn't seem all that bright, judged Kastner, slowly repeating himself in a more articulated voice, pressing his finger onto the map that he presented upside down through the lowered window. "Launay-Mal-Nommé," he specified. "That's where I'm going."

"Launay," the woman finally said without looking at the map, "I know it. It's on my way. Wait a minute and I'll tell you."

A pause, then, in a monotonous tone, a succession of first rights and first rights, of lefts before a light, of thirds after the traffic circle, you couldn't miss it; Kastner had quickly stopped following. "Listen," he said to her, "if you're heading that way, I can give you a lift if you like. You can tell me where to go. Get in—if you like." Another pause, then she gave only a small nod; as she walked around the back of the car, she said something about a bus which Kastner didn't understand. She got in, setting the bag down by her feet. It was in her way for the entire ride, but Kastner didn't dare suggest putting it on the backseat.

The ride offered a uniform vista of scattered gray houses, few of which seemed inhabited, a fair number of which were for sale—but who would want them, Kastner wondered, who would want the ones whose narrow windows didn't look out to the sea? Not me. Not really a place for me. I prefer the sun, and anyway, when you get down to it, I don't have any money. On the bloodless facades one could sometimes see traces of water from a flowerpot or hanging laundry, a sign of life that dripped from the wash and irrigated the flowers. Other facades were barely still breathing, bearing the old skins of advertisements painted fifty years before, the ghosts of hernia trusses and phosphatides.

Immobile on her seat, lips almost still, his passenger indicated the route step by step for Kastner—who, ostensibly watching the road, used his peripheral vision to take in the harsh makeup: apple-green eyelids, two violet lines under the eyebrows, two circles of terra-cotta blush on the cheeks, and extraterrestrial garnet-red lipstick. All of it against a rather pale background. His peripheral vision even made out the time on the kind of little wristwatch you can win at a local fair—something-or-other to seven— and spotted a few red traces that flaked on the half moons of chewed fingernails. Upstream from one of them, Kastner thought he identified a wedding band—but no, the object, having turned, was decorated with a cheap little green stone flanked by three brilliants.

They headed on toward Launay-Mal-Nommé; the young woman was now completely silent. To fill that silence a little, Kastner decided to divulge the reasons for his presence. Employed by a small private company, they had dispatched him into the sector with the mission of finding someone. For reasons that weren't clear to him, he specified—probably some miserable matter of debt repayment, as was too often the case. Careful not to touch his passenger, he stretched out his arm toward the glove compartment and pulled out by feel two or three photos of the someone in question. You wouldn't have seen her, by any chance? She was barely listening or didn't understand it all, said no the way she might have said yes; she didn't seem too happy or too stable. Kastner felt a certain sympathy rising in him, not far removed from a vague solidarity.

Around a bend, the young woman pointed her finger (there, I'm getting off there) at a small, isolated house near the road: Kastner braked while downshifting. The house was gray and squat, like so many others in the area, with a small garden on the side. Won over to the wild state, timorous flowers encircled a yellowed palm that, half-dead from cold despite the microclimate, looked like a large janitor's broom that had been planted in the ground and started growing. "It's not too much farther," the young woman said. "Straight ahead about another half mile."

"Thank you," said Kastner. "Thank you very much."

"Thank *you*," said the young woman. "Can I offer you something to drink?"

"I don't want to impose," said Kastner.

"Oh, come on," she said with a new little smile. Then, as she bent down to get her bag, her left hand seemingly accidentally brushed Kastner's right thigh. Who shuddered imperceptibly. Who then said sure, OK, and parked his car on the verge. "Don't leave your car out here," said the young woman. "I'll open up for you."

"Sure, OK," repeated Kastner, whose auto then crossed through the gate and rounded the house toward a small courtyard that mirrored the garden. Kastner switched off the engine, got out of the car, and slammed the door without taking his keys from the ignition.

The sea was not very far away. Through a side window, in the absence of a clear horizon line, one could almost see it blending with the sky in the waning daylight. Kastner was now sitting in a not overly comfortable wicker armchair, a glass in his hand, piles of brochures at his feet. The furnishings in the living room were rudimentary, mismatched as in the kinds of houses one rents on vacation; a socket hung bulbless from a wire in the middle of the ceiling. After a first glass, Kastner had accepted another, then a third, before the young woman had suggested, given the hour and since he was there, that he stay for dinner. It would be a change from the usual steak and fries swallowed alone and at top speed; he hadn't put up much resistance. They didn't speak much more after that. Kastner heard the woman moving glass and metal objects in the kitchen. The idea—incongruous, immediately dismissed—crossed his mind that he could spend his whole life this way.

While waiting, he took stock of the brochures: always the same magazines in last month's issues, a television guide, the almanac of tides for the current year. Leafing through the latter, he looked for today's date, scarcely familiar with these phenomena. Nonetheless, he seemed to understand that corresponding to today's date, at eleven twenty-four P.M., there would be a record level of high tide. The young woman passed through the living room from time to time, restoring the levels in the glasses until dinner was pronounced ready.

She had prepared only white foods: peeled shrimp, noodles, and plain yogurt, seasoned with sauces in tubes whose colors were no less vivid than her makeup. White wine. As Kastner asked a few questions about her life, she claimed to have worked the previous year in a canning factory, to have lost her job, to be currently unemployed, like a fair number of people in the area (unfortunately that seems to be the case all over, Kastner commiserated gravely), but that she helped out twice a week at a fish market in Ploubazlanec (I worked in fish too, Kastner informed her, without specifying further).

After dinner—rather drunk, to tell the truth—Kastner reeled out a few tortuous phrases from which one could deduce that he found the young woman quite pleasing and that he was, indeed, rather attracted to her. As she smiled while refilling his glass, he judged that the situation was advancing nicely. As she did not pull her hand away from his, he figured it was in the bag. Kissing her voraciously a bit later as he leaned against the door, he was forced to admit that he was having a hard time standing up. Then, with a snicker, his fingers blindly sought an opening in the uncooperative textile; he was starting to get excited when he broke out in a cold sweat. The woman laughed and shook her head; she gently caressed Kastner's cheek before her hand slid down to his neck, against his chest, and when she passed over his belt the man trembled from head to foot and turned pale. Then, although she was still pressed tightly against him, Kastner continued to shake. "What's wrong?" she asked in a low voice. Kastner found it hard to explain. "Come," she said, "let's get some air. It will clear your head."

"OK," said Kastner, "sure."

He hadn't paid much attention to the time passing during dinner. He was surprised that night had already fallen, so black, opaque, and dull, solid as concrete, devoid of stars as if its consistency were blocking out the celestial vault. Far off in the corner a moon just barely hung, reduced to its thinnest shaving. Scarcely out the door, Kastner put his arm around the young woman again and took the liberty, encouraged by the fresh air and the darkness, to explore matters a bit further. She did not seem to mind this development, and so Kastner was pleased. "Wait a minute," she said. "Come—we'll be more comfortable over there."

To get over there, away from the road, they took a dirt path between two artichoke patches. The young woman went ahead while Kastner followed by guesswork, stumbling to the rhythm of the potholes, disoriented by darkness, horniness, and white wine. Unable to see even his feet, the man discovered at the last second that the sea was right there, thirty yards below. You couldn't see it from the top of the cliff he had just reached, but Kastner divined its proximity by its habitual low growl, punctuated with convulsions. Crashing here and there on the rocks, a larger wave exploded like a bass drum, dissipating afterward in shudders of studded cymbal. The woman seemed to be disappearing toward the silhouette of a small blockhouse, the size of a sentry box for two—perfect, stammered Kastner's consciousness.

But an instant later she had vanished behind the pillbox. Kastner reached it, walked around it without finding her. He tried calling out to her, realizing only then that he didn't know her name, and timidly emitted a few exclamations of the *hey, hello* variety—followed by a prolonged *euhh* for his own benefit, bending toward the sea but leaning with one hand against the sentry box wall.

Then, as he tumbled into the void under the impact of a violent shove, his groan was transformed into a strangled cry, a horrified whimper that stretched out while, in fast motion, the sensations of his last dream rushed toward him. During his fall he barely had time to hope he would wake up again before hitting the ground, but not this time. This time his body would shatter for real against the rocks. Of the man named Kastner only his clothes would remain intact, transformed into a sack of broken bones. Two hours later the tide would rise to take care of them; then its record level would carry them far away from the coast, and six weeks afterward the sea would bring them back, beyond recognition.

That Jean-Claude Kastner should manage, first, to lose his way in a civilized and well-marked region already suggests that he was not the world's sharpest investigator. That he should have to ask directions of a passerby says a lot about his ingenuousness. But that he should not recognize her as the very person he was seeking disqualifies him once and for all. Even if that person had changed a lot.

The fact was, she had completely transformed herself. Judging by the documents they had given him, Kastner had pictured some tall, elegant blonde with interminable legs and high heels, the delicately pitched gait of a tightrope walker, and a clear gaze sloping gently down toward him. That was how he had visualized her. That was no longer the case. She no longer fit a single point of the description. On the other hand, it's true that, since the day she had disappeared, things had had plenty of time to evolve.

C H A P T E R 3

AND THE NEXT DAY, you are someone looking for Paul
Salvador. Your vehicle carries you toward the eastern part
of Paris, near Porte Dorée, not far from the Bois de
Vincennes. You park in front of the modern building that
houses Stochastic Films: six floors of offices and studios, sixty
million francs in yearly revenues, rising from the corner of
Avenue du Général-Dodds and Boulevard Poniatowski. You
walk in without attracting attention. Airtight as a bunker,
the lobby is decorated with green plants and lit by indirect
spots; in its center rises a tall, polychromatic abstract sculpture, a totem planted slantwise in a gravel doormat. To the
right, a row of exceptional receptionists, all nails, lashes, and
breasts; to the left, nothing special. Just ahead, the elevators. Forget the receptionists, head straight for the elevators.

You cross the lobby; no one asks you anything. Secure
in their three-day beards, the young men in boots and
leather jackets barely even jostle you. Your eyes would also
like to linger on all the unstructured girls who come and
go here, but you ignore them as well and proceed straight
ahead. You enter the elevator, press number 3.

The elevator door opens onto a hallway that you follow to the first open office: that's it. Enter. Stand quietly in a corner. Wait. Whatever happens, no one will notice you. In any case, Salvador's office is empty for the moment. It's a large room whose double-thick panes calmly overlook the avenue traffic. Armchairs and conference table, as well as large oval mirror and sofa. On one wall, two paintings by who knows who; against another, volume lowered, six stacked televisions broadcast the day's programs. The walls are dark green, the carpet warm sand. Not a folder lying around, not a sheet of paper; all the data is digitized. Only on the table do a few files rest, ongoing projects that Stochastic will deliver, made-to-order and ready-to-wear, to public and private TV stations.

And here comes Salvador, seeming not very busy. He walks around his office, stares at but doesn't really see the specters wriggling onscreen, nor the avenue through the window, nor his reflection in the oval mirror. Distractedly he leafs through the files while awaiting his assistant. Here she is now. Let's go.

37-24-36: no matter what the season, Donatienne stands out by wearing clothes that are supernaturally short and miraculously low-cut, sometimes so short and so low-cut at the same time that between these adjectives almost no actual fabric remains. Endowed with the energy of a breeder reactor, Donatienne throws an envelope quilted with plastic bubbles onto the table before dropping into a chair and expressing herself in a rapid voice, sharp but fragile like a fishbone made of chalk. It sometimes happens that talking, for Donatienne, consists in reeling off a single, unending sentence without catching her breath, without period or comma or pause—a performance that, as far as Salvador can tell, only Roland Kirk has matched on the saxophone, and perhaps also Johnny Griffin to a lesser extent

—all the while beating, in triple time, the arm of the chair with her right palm. It also happens that once in a while she speaks more soberly.

Salvador rips open the envelope that she dropped on the table. It contains two 45s recorded five or six years earlier, when vinyl was still the coin of the realm. Both carry the name Gloria Stella in boldface, followed by the title of the A-side ("Excessive" for one, "We're Not Taking Off" for the other) superimposed over a color photo of the singer. Donatienne, meanwhile, describes all the trouble she's had procuring these two records, now out of print. She seems to be stressing—Salvador is barely listening—the gap between the breadth of her research and the value of its object. To underscore her point, she makes a disdainful gesture with her left hand while shrugging one shoulder, causing a strap of her brief garment to slip down the other shoulder. As she frequently shrugs her shoulders, a strap of her dress slips one time out of two, and the next time it's the other strap; Salvador averts his eyes two times out of two. But just then the telephone rings, allowing him to busy himself elsewhere. "I'm listening," he utters.

At the other end of the line, Jouve sounds concerned. The evening before, his employee Kastner neglected to call in with a progress report, as he was instructed to do daily, no matter what, and fruitful or not. "I'm a little worried," he says. "That's the first time. It isn't like him. Anyway, I'll see if he calls tonight."

"All right," says Salvador. "Keep me posted." Then, after hanging up, "To work," he says. Donatienne opens the Gloria Stella file.

Usually, Salvador's programs appeal to collective memory. Where are they now? That's the formula: a good, reliable formula that has proven itself time and time again. You go in search of a name whose posterity has faded, whose echo has died out. Retired talk-show host, single-role actor, overachieving crook, radio game-show champion, vanished top-of-the-bill amnestied by memory. You exhume a one-time instant celebrity who had soon dissolved into neglect, someone people remember so little that they don't even remember having forgotten him, but who is there nonetheless: stored like the others at the back of a closet, in memory's oldest boxes. Those boxes are still there, way in back, even though a few have been damaged by a leak in memory's ceiling. The labels pasted on them are now a bit hard to read. Salvador's programs consist in repainting the ceiling, refreshing the memory, opening those boxes.

But this might take a more intimate and personal turn. So it was, for example, with *From the Bottom of My Heart,* a ratings hit with the pre-retirement crowd in the provinces, or with *The Prettiest Girl on the Beach* ("You once saw the prettiest girl on the beach and you remember her. You remember her all too well, though you didn't dare talk to her. Do you remember her name? Write to us. We'll find you that prettiest girl on your beach"). It was another matter entirely with Gloria Stella, whose case fell into a broader category. Indeed, first as a popular singer, then as the heroine of human interest stories, she had gotten herself pretty well noticed five or six years ago, for a few months.

Career brief: Born Gloire Abgrall, precocious teenage fashion model. Entered the world of variety shows under the pseudonym dreamed up by Gilbert Flon, her lover-cum-agent.

Bottom line: those two 45s, a shot at the Olympia, a few tours as special guest star, number three on the hit parade for "Excessive"; photographs, autographs, fan club, movies on the horizon. It all looked very promising until Gilbert Flon took a suspicious dive down a fourth-floor elevator shaft.

Since then: suspicion, investigation, prosecution witnesses, indictment, trial, verdict (five years; extenuating circumstances), prison, release for good conduct, disappearance.

So that, having covered the ground in the teenage weeklies, then in the women's monthlies, having cleared herself a little place in the Arts and Entertainment sections of the dailies, it was more and more in black-and-white that they then transferred her from the Celebrity news to the Legal columns, before she sank into the deep column of Forgotten.

Where, indeed, was she now? Not a peep in four years. She must be thirty by now. The perceptible path of Gloire Abgrall stopped dead the day of her release from prison, the date on which any relatives and allies she had left stopped receiving the slightest sign of life from her. She disappeared into the woodwork like a good thousand other persons a year who are never seen again. Still, Salvador and Donatienne are hopeful. While waiting for Jouve's men to find her, they put the finishing touches on their project: specifying the order of documents from the video library, archives, news of the day, interviews with those closest, specialists' viewpoints—courts, mental health, and show business.

Naturally, Salvador is not the first to look for Gloire Abgrall. Numerous paparazzi have tried, with no other result than, for one who was a little more brazen than the rest, the outline of his body deeply embossed in the roof of a Peugot parked in front of Rouen cathedral (Seine-Maritime region), at the bottom of a two-hundred-foot drop.

After their work has ended and Donatienne has left, Salvador makes the rounds of his office one last time. Noticing, next to its envelope, the recorded opus of Gloria Stella, he slips a 45 from its pouch and drops "Excessive" onto the turntable. Standing near the window he watches, on the boulevard, a leather-clad woman extricating herself from a diesel automobile. The song plays and he listens to the words, popping the envelope's little plastic bubbles between his fingers, one by one, the way he had treated, on family vacations thirty years before, the little bubbles of algae growing on the submerged rocks off the Giens peninsula (Var region).

C H A P T E R 4

ON THE MORNING OF THAT SAME DAY, the woman who had sealed Jean-Claude Kastner's fate awoke a little before nine o'clock. She had opened her eyes on the grayish ceiling, then, recognizing it, got up and slipped on a shapeless green fleece-lined bathrobe. But immediately afterward, in the bathroom mirror, she had trouble recognizing her face.

Hurling a man into the void being the sort of thing that can make you forget to remove your makeup, it was a contracted mask that appeared to her in the glass, petrified by sweat and suffocating under the greasepaint. She restored her image with scant consideration, using cold water and household soap, as delicately as one sandblasts a facade. Her hair was not a pretty sight, but she, who hardly cared, brushed it back violently. She gave the mirror an evil grimace that bared her teeth, which she then brushed no less brutally—until her gums bled, the handle of the toothbrush snapped in two, and the young woman swore out loud while spitting a pinkish froth onto the sink's yellowed enamel. She rinsed her mouth endlessly before putting on new makeup that was only slightly more discreet than the day before, tying her hair with a brown rubber band. Back in her room, she haphazardly chose a sky-blue blouse with feather prints and a bright red skirt, throwing a large navy-blue smock over the whole thing.

Standing in the kitchen, Gloire Abgrall then emptied a large bowl of coffee in one gulp. On the sides of the bowl, pochoir silhouettes of fruits and vegetables chased after each other beneath the cracks. She glanced out the window to check the weather: silent light-gray front. The windows hadn't been cleaned in some time, and it was hard to make out what was happening outside, but even in the kitchen it wasn't that easy to see either, as if the air itself hadn't been cleaned. Setting the bowl on the table, she then gathered some food scraps onto a page of newspaper—crusts, tops, peelings—before going out.

Behind the house, the back of the small courtyard ended in a shed in which a one-eyed, formerly white Renault R5 stood parked, and a few rimless tires, two caneless chairs, and an enucleated lamp grew mold. A first-generation washing machine and an antique boiler framed a hutch in which a rabbit, fleshy and trembling, pondered the short term with an opaque eye. The young woman crossed the courtyard with her food, a grating little wind brushing at her temples. Then, as she was about to lean toward the animal: "Personally," said Beliard, "I don't disapprove."

Gloire Abgrall turned her head and Beliard was there, sitting on her shoulder. Well, what do you know, he was back. Casually posed on her shoulder, legs dangling and eyes looking elsewhere, Beliard leaned with one hand on her collarbone, and with the other rubbed his chin.

"Ah," she breathed, "there you are." Beliard nodded contentedly. "And anyway, so what?" she said. "Disapprove of what?"

Beliard crossed his tiny legs and doubled over with a sharp laugh: "The guy last night," he said. "Others might disapprove. Not me. You were within your rights, Gloire, you've had enough to deal with. They've given you enough to deal with. I'm just calling it as I see it."

"I don't give a shit how you see it," Gloire declared.

"It's my duty to tell you," Beliard observed in a pinched voice. "It's part of my job. Afterward, you can do as you like." Then he fell silent, sulkily folding his arms and staring straight ahead.

"All right, fine," said the young woman, "don't pout."

"I am *not* pouting," Beliard said coldly. "If you only knew how little I cared."

"Come on now," she said. "Come on now, Beliard."

Beliard is a skinny little brunette, about a foot tall and with a slightly receding hairline, part on the side, drooping eyelids and upper lip, muddy complexion. He is wearing a brown cotton suit, dark purple tie, and shiny little brown shoes, spit-polished. Rather disgraceful spineless face, though with a determined expression. Arms folded, his fingers stick out of sleeves that are a bit too long for him, and drum on his elbows.

At best, Beliard is an illusion. At best he is an hallucination forged by the young woman's deranged mind. At worst, he is a kind of guardian angel, or at least can claim some kinship with that congregation. Let us envision the worst.

If he really is one, created too ugly and too small to be officially recognized by a fraternity overly preoccupied with its movie-star physique, they must immediately have dumped him on Social Services. That is, unless they simply abandoned him on the side of a highway during a move, a parade, or an angels' convention abroad, cuffed with his standard-issue halo to a roadsign. Whatever the case, from a very young age he had to get along by himself, taking advantage (despite everything) of whatever gifts and qualities his birth conferred. Ignored by his own kind, renounced by his hierarchy, perhaps even slapped with a professional ban, he is compelled to practice his trade as a freelancer, outside normal channels and as discreetly as possible.

Moreover, he isn't always there, or at least not always physically present: the frequency and duration of his visits with the young woman vary. Sometimes he stays away for two months, sometimes he shows up every evening like a regular at the local bar, sometimes for two hours in the middle of the night as if with some girl. Always he seems rather self-centered, not too observant of principles, often in a surly mood. Occasionally he keeps office hours, a cruising little nine-to-five, but he might also spend three weeks grounded on his little corner of shoulder, immobile, nervous, taciturn, looking hunted, as if hidden away or wanted by the authorities. In short, he's pretty irregular. The only general rule is that he shows up when Gloire is alone, which has not been an uncommon occurrence in the past four years. Lately he hasn't been too constant, coming by only two or three times a week. Not that he does anything in particular when he's there, but at least he's there.

At the moment, he was clearing his throat, patting his lips with a balled-up handkerchief. He seemed to be lost in thought. "Did it feel the same?" he said in a distracted voice, without looking at the young woman.

"What do you mean?" she said in the same tone. "Did what feel the same?"

"The guy last night," specified Beliard. "When you pushed him. What did it feel like? Compared to the other times, I mean."

"Fucking little asshole!" hissed Gloire. "Goddam little asshole piece of shit! We agreed we'd never bring that up."

"Just doing my job," Beliard reminded her.

As Gloire leaned toward the hutch, Beliard, to keep his balance, slid toward the back of her shoulder, almost to the shoulder blade. When she stood up again without warning, he nearly went tumbling head over heels, but regained his equilibrium just in time: "Ah," he grated, "*that* was smart." Then, having settled in again, "So, what's the plan for today?"

"You'll see," said Gloire.

"I'd like to be a little more involved in the decision-making," Beliard declared energetically. "I'd like to have my say in all this. I mean, after all, that's what I'm here for, isn't it?" She, having turned around, now walked resolutely toward the house. "Hey, what are you up to?" he worried. "Where are you going like that?"

"I have to take a piss," Gloire said abruptly, "and maybe a shit, too. I don't know yet."

"All right," said Beliard, averting his gaze, pinching and knotting his nostrils and brow. "Fine. I'll just step out for a moment."

"Now there's an idea," said Gloire.

As soon as he had evaporated, she automatically brushed off his spot with the tips of her fingers, as if to dust herself off when there wasn't anything to dust, the immaterial Beliard neither leaving any remains—spit-out fingernail, sweat, textile debris—nor having any weight on her shoulder.

He returned to his position around noon, as Gloire was getting rid of the last traces of Jean-Claude Kastner. He had watched her work, at first grumbling in a low voice, then shutting himself up in a meditative silence, without offering the slightest opinion or advice: miniservice. The day passed, waned. Late in the afternoon, Gloire settled into a folding chair under the palm tree, intending to leaf through some magazines. The dried palm leaves surrounding the tree's lower hemisphere clacked like wooden rattles, or the way a band of feverish birds might shiver with the tips of their beaks. Not so easy to read with that idiot sitting on your shoulder and naturally reading along with you—and to make matters worse, not necessarily at the same speed: "Hang on a minute," he said once as Gloire was about to turn the page, "just two seconds, all right? OK, you can turn now." Then, when night had fallen: "Well," he said, suddenly shivering, "I should start thinking about leaving soon."

"You're right," said Gloire, glancing at her watch, "you'll have to start getting ready."

Beliard shook himself, stretched, then gave a long yawn. Sighing contentedly after his yawn, not seeming especially eager to move, he stared at the setting sun, blinking his eyes as if he'd just awoken, going over events in his head, doublechecking the rest of the plan. These days he always left at about the same time—and as for where he went, the subject was never broached. If he hadn't been incorporeal, he probably would have asked for a cup of coffee, or one for the road. But in his state of substance, he had never yet shown the least sign of hunger or thirst. "Well," he finally murmured, "I'm off."

After his evaporation, Gloire spends a typical evening alone. Serves herself some wine, some bread and butter—the first is hard because it's a day old, the second because it has just come out of the fridge. Chili heated in the can, yogurt with exotic fruit flavors that she eats without transition, mechanically, while standing up, taking no more of a pause than the soundtrack of spots, jingles, and flashes spewed out by the radio. Sometimes in a low voice, an octave down, she picks up the refrain of a song. Cursory dishwashing before turning off the radio and switching on the television, which she can't bring herself to watch.

Impossible to watch it, as if Gloire had forgotten how. A TV movie starts, which she forces herself to follow to the bitter end—but it was just the opening sequence, the movie is really only starting now; that's discouraging. She tries to concentrate on the plot, but in vain: as nothing in her retains them, the images pass through her like X-rays, like an undifferentiated electronic wind, monochromatic and smooth, tepid and muted. Gloire summons the strength to switch off the TV before total hypnosis sets in.

Silence. A glance at the alarm clock creeping grudgingly toward ten P.M. Outside, not a single animal around to give a sign of life, not a single car passes on the road. Only a deafening silence in which all kinds of parasitic thoughts, a word, a name, an incoherent refrain of words and names, develop and become amplified: an insane melodic loop whose echo comes and goes, distorts and twists around, as if in a machine drum, in Gloire's mind as she sits in front of nothing. To break out of it she turns the radio on full-blast, then immediately snaps it off again, horrified. She gets up, walks a few feet only to sit down somewhere else; every evening it's the same thing. Ten thirty and no desire to go to sleep despite the spread of multicolored soporifics splayed out next to her bed, asking only to be of service. Suddenly Gloire stands and grabs the collar of her coat.

She heads to the Manchester, only ten minutes away with the Renault. It's the kind of rural nightclub that you sometimes find on the fringes of small towns, sometimes even in the middle of the countryside; the kind that make you wonder what they're doing there. Inside the straw hut made of concrete is just a bar that closes a bit late, containing a small floor on which the only dancer, two mornings a week, is a cleaning woman with a broom. This evening there's no one at the Manchester except three young guys busy making noise near the bar. The young guys resemble each other like brothers, sporting bomber jackets and wide French-made jeans, tow-colored hair, and checkered shirts. They are the crossbred product of farmers, workers, and fishermen, and two of the three are unemployed; Gloire doesn't know them. She orders a drink, standing not too far from these guys who have already had a few drinks themselves. As one of them, the tallest one, begins talking to her rather familiarly, the two others split their sides in the background. We gather she doesn't much care for such behavior.

Indeed, she is not in the mood and things could turn ugly, at least for the tall guy who has moved nearer and is now trying to put his arm around her. Lucky for him, not far away, nonchalant as you please, Beliard, who is invisibly keeping an eye on all this, is not about to stand idly by and let Gloire unleash her violence again so readily. Extra hours and overtime rates, but no matter—the homunculus decides to step in.

CHAPTER 5

DONATIENNE REAPPEARED THE FOLLOWING AFTERNOON, dying of thirst. The weather had changed (light drizzle), and Donatienne had changed too. This wasn't immediately noticeable but, after she had shed her raincoat, what she was wearing revealed itself to be still scantier than the day before—so short and so low-cut that this time these adjectives tended to blend together, with a view toward shacking up in the same entry of the first dictionary they could find.

In a corner of his office, Salvador had a small refrigerator containing all the necessary accoutrements, but as for glasses he possessed only cups of the disposable picnic variety. And the sound of ice cubes in the plastic was dull, cheap, without resonance, without the elation of real glass glasses, in which the ice may clink and glint proudly: the gin and tonic's rhythm section.

"Too bad," Donatienne resigned herself. "Did Jouve call?" Salvador shook his head. "Call him," Donatienne suggested.

Salvador called, but the line was busy. "I'll try again later," he said.

Before him, in scattered folders and envelopes, lay his main project: tall blonde women in the movies, in the arts in general, and more broadly, in life. Their histories, their characters, their roles. Their specialties and their variations. Their whole significance in five-times-fifty-two minutes. While the project mainly involved splicing together existing works, the fifth episode was to be devoted to a specific case. They had sought out a living example of a bizarre tall blonde, eventually settling on Gloire Abgrall.

Indeed, after they had reviewed all the classical formats, Gloire embodied, by her evolution, her life, and her work, a special case within the framework. She could represent the anomaly, the oddity, the indirect example, one way among many to illustrate Salvador's thesis—to wit, that tall blondes constituted a group apart, neither better nor worse than anyone else but special, governed by specific laws, following a separate plan: an irreducible category of humanity. In short, tall blondes versus the rest of the world. A firm conviction, an obvious postulate in Salvador's mind, but somewhat difficult to demonstrate. Every day new arguments presented themselves to his brain, and every day he struggled to shape them, to establish the overall order in all of this. For Donatienne, once more, he tried to clarify his thinking.

"OK," said Donatienne, "I can see this hasn't progressed very far. Don't you want to try Jouve again?" He tried: still busy. "Let's just go there," proposed Donatienne. "The best thing would be to just go there. I'll drive."

They took Porte d'Ivry to reach the left bank of the Seine and followed it in a westerly direction. In a car with Donatienne, life itself became convertible. As on the previous day, she couldn't stop talking, her uninterrupted discourse standing in for the car radio. Moreover, once past the Pont Neuf they had to take several tunnels—that series of short, cold, underground passageways that border the river—and at the entrance to each tunnel her voice progressively faded out, her words stopping until they had come out the other side: a phenomenon car radios know all too well. Then her outpouring resumed as soon as they were back in daylight, but without picking up where it had left off, having continued underground in suspension, probably as an interior monologue. Salvador then had to splice the two halves together, to reconstruct the buried missing portion.

Ten bridges later, near Bir-Hakeim, they turned left into the fifteenth arrondissement: a boulevard, an avenue, then a maze of small, quiet streets up to Jouve's building behind the Kinopanorama. One of those small, quiet, distinguished streets that knows how to behave, whose dapper, freshly remodeled buildings never raise their voices inconsiderately. Parking lot, entrance code, intercom, elevator, doorbell, spyhole (dark for two seconds), bolt.

Then Jouve, looking rather tired. "Ah," he said, "it's you." Voice sluggish and motor functions circumspect, with perhaps a hint of anisette. His eyes kept watch as best they could above their ringed sockets, ready to sink into them and go back to sleep. "Still no news from my field man," he immediately informed them. "But come in, come in." They moved into the living room: geometric wallpaper and skin-pink vase containing a potted flower; a few paintings on the walls (wedding scene in Charente, full-length portrait of a puffin); distinct undertone of Airwick eucalyptus. At Salvador and Donatienne's entrance, a weeping Mrs. Jouve rose from her end of the sofa to turn off the VCR and briefly greeted them before leaving the room. Salvador had already met her; Donatienne, who came in after him, saw only a thin, translucent silhouette, hypersensitive and hypertense.

"She's been watching TV all day," Jouve apologized. "She gets very emotional about the soaps. You'll have something to drink?"

Motioning toward two armchairs, he dropped onto the other end of the couch, facing the television that he designated with a brief movement of his chin. "Not always the same taste," he sighed. In fact, on either side of the sofa lay two remotes: while Jouve measured out the pastis, Donatienne imagined the remote control wars every evening in front of the TV.

"I have to say, I'm a bit surprised," Jouve reiterated. "This isn't like Kastner. We'll wait another day or two."

"It's just that we can't let it drag on too long," Salvador worried. "Don't you have anyone who's a little more competent?"

Jouve stared at his glass as he thought. His glance always drifted very slowly toward things, then adhered to them, stuck there, seemed to have trouble becoming unglued.

"How about Personnettaz?" suggested Salvador. "Couldn't we try with him? He was really good."

Jouve continued to examine his glass before dragging his eyes away, with the sound of tape being ripped off cardboard, and training them on Salvador.

"I'd rather not bother him for so little," he finally said. "I'd prefer to put someone else on it first. Maybe Boccara; I'll call him later on. If that doesn't work, then we could try Personnettaz."

Night was falling when they left Jouve's. After they'd had a little something at the restaurant at Invalides station, Donatienne returned home, but Salvador didn't. A taxi carried him to Porte Dorée. No one left at that hour at Stochastic: in place of the receptionists, under an anemic spotlight, there was only a young watchman rubbing his eyes over a Xerox of international law. "That's not enough light, Lestiboudois," Salvador said in a paternal voice. "Go get a lamp. You'll ruin your eyes that way."

Having returned to his office with the idea of working a bit, Salvador gave up the idea fairly easily. Hardly had he poured himself a few fingers than he began drinking and undressing, a sip, a piece of clothing, a sip, another piece of clothing, such that the glass and he became, at the same moment, respectively empty and nude. That done, he opened a closet and pulled out a blanket, which he spread over the couch before slipping under it in the company of a book entitled *How to Disappear Completely and Never Be Found* by Doug Richmond (New York: Citadel Press, 1994). But scarcely had he opened the work than he shut it again, pressed the switch, and six seconds later he was asleep.

CHAPTER 6

ONE CAN ENVISION SLEEP IN VARIOUS FORMS. Gray scarf, smokescreen, sonata. Gliding flight of a great pale bird, open green portal. Plains. But also slipknot, asphyxiating gas, bass clarinet. Insect retracted onto its brief life, final warning before repossession. Rampart. It's a matter of style; it depends on the way each one sleeps or doesn't sleep, on the dreams that scare or spare one.

At the moment, everyone is sleeping. Salvador, on his couch, poorly. Donatienne, tossing in her huge square bed. Jouve next to Mrs. Jouve, soundly. Jean-Claude Kastner, definitively. As for the woman who hurled Kastner into the big night, judging from the tubes of benzodiazepines and buspirone hydrochloride scattered over her nightstand, she is sleeping chemically. She snores a bit from time to time. She has left a lamp lit nearby, or maybe she simply neglected to turn it off. At the foot of her bed a few books lie open, one on top of the other: detective novels, works by Freud in mass-market paperbacks, and a series of small volumes in English devoted to the identification of common birds, European trees, and wildflowers. In the shadows, not far away, sit an empty flask of cheap rum, a half-empty liter of cane syrup, and a full ashtray. It is the same every night; nothing seems to change very much. Since Kastner's visit, only two small things are different: one on Gloire's body and the other on the table.

On one of the young woman's ankles, a large Band-Aid protects a cut dating from the day before yesterday, as she was getting rid of Kastner's car after emptying it of its contents: rags, bungee cords, tools, and minor spare items, old rubbish from the glove compartment, Jean-Claude Kastner's personal effects and vehicular registration, which she had gathered in a box—except for two tools, the pliers and hammer. Except, too, for the pouch in which Kastner had kept his itinerary, photographs, and road maps. The pouch isn't bad. Emptied, its contents burned in the sink, washed and disinfected, it now rests on the table.

Behind the wheel of the thus-cleaned car, Gloire had then taken the road to Tréguier and deposited the box in the town incinerator, after which she headed north, the pliers and hammer resting on the seat next to her. Past Larmor, another bit of cliff overhung a very deep ditch, filled with water no matter what the tide. The promontory was relatively steep, rarely visited—ideal. Gloire had parked the car facing the void, using the pliers to remove the plates and the hammer to erase the engine and chassis numbers. Then she had lowered the windows, released the handbrake, and pushed with all her might. In vain, at first: the vehicle resisted. Then, after having moved an inch, slowly another inch, it had suddenly accelerated as of its own volition, to get it over with, and everything had gone smoothly—although at the last moment the young woman's leg had gotten caught in the bumper, an end of which had scraped her ankle. Gloire had cried out and cursed rudely as the car foundered. Bent forward, holding her ankle in one hand, she had leaned grimacing over the cliff. Then as she watched the vehicle sink her face had grown calmer: as if she were under anaesthesia; as if the fall of bodies brought her some peace, like Anthony Perkins pondering the same spectacle in 1960—except that Kastner's vehicle was a compact beige Renault registered in the Paris suburbs that immersed itself obediently and without a fuss, while Janet Leigh's had been a big white recalcitrant Ford, license number NFB 418.

Then she returned home on foot, limping, following the coastal paths dotted with red and white lines painted on boulders and markers. She buried the plates between two stone blocks, under a mattress of gravel. Back at the house, she had bandaged her ankle and then, while she was at it, converted the pouch into a new medicine kit.

She is still asleep. She does not move in her slumber, even though in her dream, for hours, she has been straddling a powerful motorcycle. Day breaks imperceptibly. Day breaks slowly, delicately, the way an illuminated Boeing softly leaves the runway, the way a string orchestra begins the last movement.

But soon this movement ends and the sun shines, motionless. Gloire climbs down from her motorcycle. She heads toward a phone booth, and it's then that she awakens. Eyes wide open, she remains still for a moment before confronting yet another day: she gets up and puts on her hideous green bathrobe. The kitchen, the electric coffee pot. As the coffee drips, the young woman's gaze falls on a sheet of yellow paper, the back of a flyer lying on a corner of the table with a drawing on it that she must have sketched the evening before—she doesn't remember very clearly. It's the embryo of a portrait, somewhat shaky, perhaps even (worst of all) a self-portrait. Whatever it is, Gloire immediately rips it up with her eyes shut, rips it again into minuscule squares which she dumps into the toilet bowl, flushing them down without looking.

In the bathroom, two tiles are missing on the floor of the shower, a third is cracked, and the rest are coated with tan and brown grit. Gloire has hung her bathrobe on the hook screwed in behind the door. She is naked in front of the square mirror above the sink, a mirror too small to let her see her body, which she has no desire to see in any case. No desire to see her long, flawless legs, her high, round, firm breasts and high, round, firm buttocks that, decked out in their tracksuit, Jean-Claude Kastner would never have imagined. Had he envisioned such a body, Kastner would never have dared to desire it.

She washes quickly, practically a cold shower, before slowly putting on her makeup. A first layer of moisturizer followed by an almost white base coat, applied evenly the way one prepares a canvas. Having penciled her eyes in almond, she repaints her lids turquoise. Then with the help of a chrome device like snail tongs, Gloire accentuates the curve of her eyelashes before making them very dark and very thick with very greasy mascara. Soon her eyes are the only living things in this face; only they show movement in this immobile mask. Gray-green, they shift from green to gray depending on weather, place, light, and mood. After that, outlining her lips with a red crayon, she overruns the edges, then saturates the inside with a brush. Two orange circles on her cheeks, two swipes of a black pencil on the arches of her eyebrows, and that's that. Beneath this makeup, Gloire Abgrall could pass for a circus performer committed after a nervous breakdown—but not too depressed to perform her little skit as part of the festival organized, family members in attendance, for open house day at the clinic.

We can understand how Gloire, a woman on the run, would wish to disguise herself, how such a mask would help make her unrecognizable; but we might wonder nonetheless whether making herself ugly doesn't also afford her a certain pleasure. Thus bedizened, inspecting her face in the mirror until she feels like vomiting, she is in fact quite content—exulting, guffawing, grimacing— and her contentment increases tenfold when she hears herself utter a few obscenities in an unusually shrill register.

Moreover, that excess of makeup must rub off when someone kisses her—but hardly anyone kisses her, she makes sure of that. Of course, she occasionally finds herself obliged: to get rid of Kastner, for example, no way to avoid it. And indeed, then it rubs off but good. Kastner never saw himself after the kiss, falling into the dark void joyously smeared with garnet, apple green, and brown.

Now Gloire has calmed down a little. She has just noticed a groundswell of light gold threatening the roots of her drab hair. Remember to color it this weekend. Change the Band-Aid. Find something to put on. Strap that watch to her wrist: a quarter to ten. Hey, and what about Beliard? Still naked as a jaybird, Gloire lights a cigarette along with the television, for television in the morning is just as stiff as gin on an empty stomach. But she dresses before the set as if it were someone. She slips on another of her impossible getups: a jacquard decorated with hoarfrost crystals and green, yellow, and mauve bear cubs on a chiné background, over a pair of navy-blue sweatpants crimped at the ankles.

On the television, a female newscaster reports that old people who drink wine have 27 percent better reasoning capacity than old people who don't. Good news for the wine industry, the newscaster comments, and Gloire wonders if that gloss is unintentional humor or not. She ties back her hair, puts on her glasses. A harsh glint in her eyes flashes over the lenses; she is frightening to look at.

Another flash of pale sunlight crosses the dusty window-pane toward the unmade bed, making the rumpled sheets look even dirtier than they are. It is now almost cold in the room; Gloire summarily straightens her bed to warm up the atmosphere. Then she goes out to check the contents of the mailbox: not much, various flyers and papers that she discards without looking at them, keeping only an envelope with the letterhead of the Bardo law firm on rue de Tilsitt, Paris, which contains a check signed with the name Lagrange. Ten thirty, eleven fifteen, Beliard really is late today. In his stead, someone knocks at the kitchen window: Alain.

Alain, a retired sailor in the fifty-five range, looking less knowledgeable than his age would warrant. Compact, not very tall, face made of scarlet box calf, Gitanes-blue eyes and short reddish hair. V-neck pullover, pants of the same faded blue. Limps a bit because of an accident, but remains stable on his short lower limbs.

Alain stops in on Gloire from time to time, gladly lets himself be served two little glasses of rum, chats with her about benign subjects, the weather, the tide, the locals, the shopkeepers; sometimes he brings her a fish. A big one or a little one, depending. When he smiles, the wrinkles bunch up around his eyes. Though willingly talkative, he speaks in a hesitant, almost interrogative tone and, because of another accident, the movements of his lips are not entirely synchronized with his words. Such as: "How's it going, Christine?"

"Going OK," said Gloire, "going OK. Want some coffee?"

This time, Alain puts on the table a midsize mullet—not the best fish in the world, mullet, but what can you do? Then he talks about the weather, which he deems normal for the season, then about the tide, which was exceptional the other day, as we know, over 380, nearly 400.

This phenomenon comes, he informs her, from the align-
ment of the earth with the moon and the sun. It's what
they call a syzygy.

"A what?" says Gloire.

"A syzygy," repeats Alain, who throws his head back
the more briskly to down his coffee. Then come several
familiar memories of his travels and more precisely of
Australia. Australia where, Alain assures her, not so long
ago they still ate their steaks with jelly. From there he forks
off onto other fleshly preparations, generalizes about edi-
ble meats, then about the controversial personality of the
local butcher.

"And is he a good butcher?" Gloire pretends to care,
she who lives mainly on dairy, canned goods, vegetables,
an egg in a crepe, or nothing.

"He knows what he's doing," says Alain. "He's good."

He reflects a bit before developing his thought, an
opportunity Gloire seizes to pour him a little more coffee.

"He's good," Alain continues, "but how can I put it?
The animals are always a bit, with respect to what one
would like, always a bit too old, that's it. You ask for lamb,
you get mutton."

Gloire smiles, then snickers nervously.

"You go for veal," Alain pursues, "he just about gives you
its mother. He prepares a good cut of meat, got nothing to
say against that, but he likes to take them a little aged."

Gloire has begun to laugh in silence, in small, irrepressible waves that soon begin to swell dangerously; that
rise, curl, and finally crash before the sailor's uncompre-
hending eyes. Now Gloire hiccups, unable to stop. Alain
tries to intervene, but with her hand she desperately sig-
nals him to be quiet. "Stop," she goes between two spasms,
"stop, please stop. Shut up. Get out." Unnerved by this
familiarity, the other stops talking, stares at her curiously,

then makes up his mind to leave. He leaves, brooding. He knew she wasn't entirely normal, but to *that* extent...

He goes on his way, toward his little home which is not far from Gloire's. In his concern Alain fails to notice the metallic blue-gray Volvo 360 parked in front of her house. Body pearly with dew, windows smothered with mist, it seems that there is no one inside. But, equipped with a case of Vittel, a carton of Pall Malls, and a radiophone, someone *is* inside.

CHAPTER 7

THAT RADIOPHONE CRACKLED A BIT, but it worked:
"Boccara here," went a voice. "Can you hear me?"

"Roger," said Jouve. "That was fast. Are you sure it's
her? All right, I'll tell the client. Don't move, just wait for
my instructions. What's that? Yes, I know it's cold out.
Bundle up."

The day began at around nine o'clock. Continental
climate. After having made an appointment with Personnettaz—noon at the office—Jouve had put on his coat to
cross the city in a southwest-northeast diagonal, by Metro.
At the Botzaris stop he got out to take a wide, calm street
of provincial character, bordered by plane trees and surrounded by private villas, with few passersby and few
shops: walking toward a small police station, Jouve skirted a modest hairdresser's salon, an empty pharmacy, a
grade school, and the headquarters of some charity orga-
nizations and general contractors.

A rather humble police station served the Amérique
quarter. A graceless building in need of renovation, windows with rusty grates, flea-ridden facade in the middle of

which the three colors of a dirty national flag, twisted around the pole like an old curtain, overlapped each other. An insignificant outpost far removed from worldly affairs —only debutant officers must have been assigned here, or officers on the verge of retirement, or those found guilty and demoted. The main door had all the allure of a service entrance. Jouve pushed it open.

They seemed to have made some small effort since his last visit, bought a few sticks of secondhand furniture and painted the reception area green; in any case, Jouve didn't visit often. Behind a sort of counter, a young functionary recorded complaints on a fat typewriter which seemed to date from before the advent of electricity. Jouve awaited his turn on a bench while gazing over the bulletins tacked onto corkboards, skimming the map of the arrondissement, pondering two wanted posters, and lending an ear to the various plaintiffs.

Among the latter, a civvie with a short, nervous beard was complaining that a taxi driver had added, after the fact, a large 5 before the number 100 on a check for a hundred francs.

"Didn't you write out the amount?" queried the functionary.

"No," went the other, confused. "Just the number."

"Shouldn't do that," scolded the policeman. "Shouldn't ever do that. Anyway, it's against fiscal regulations."

Then a beautiful young woman with a perm, sunglasses, and tanned shoulders, the kind who drives an Austin Mini, reported to the intimidated policeman the disappearance of her Austin Mini. Jouve, waiting, studied her from top to bottom. Then, when it was his turn: "I'm here to see Inspector Clauze," he said.

"Second floor, room twelve," said the policeman.

"I know," said Jouve. They hadn't repainted the stairway.

Nor the offices. At least not number twelve, in which the guilty and demoted Inspector Clauze presented the terrier-like face of a French character actor. Sinuous voice and filament of mustache, eye squinting over slantwise smile that displayed as frankly as you please the personality of a complete phony. The perfect picture of the kind of backstabbing little crud you might see hanging around casting departments: sarcastic, obsequious, sometimes dangerous, believing himself to be clever, moreover often being so, more than you'd suspect, but ultimately not quite clever enough, since his schemes always manage to backfire. The kind they'd hire to play the shady stockbroker, blackmailing former colleague, or brother-in-law cop. And in fact, he *was* the brother-in-law cop. "So how's Genevieve?"

"She's just fine," said Jouve, "just fine. But you know how emotional she gets."

"Sure do," Clauze said with satisfaction. "And to what do I owe the honor?"

Jouve told him about Gloire Abgrall's disappearance, mentioned her two identities. Clauze was at first hardpressed to remember, then:

"Oh, right, the singer—I remember the trial. Whatever became of her?"

"That's the point," said Jouve. "I'm asking *you.*"

As usual, Clauze started waving his arms around and rolling his eyes heavenward. "Always the same," he summarized, "you know damn well I can't do anything for you. She paid her debt, all right? You can look for a missing person when it's a minor, but for adults there's nothing we can do. Adults have every right to disappear."

"Robert," uttered Jouve.

"Even when it's the family who's looking, you know it never works out. If somebody doesn't want to be found, there's nothing we can do. Nothing I can do."

"Forget about that," said Jouve, "find me everything you can about her, Robert. Find it now."

"Careful how you talk to me," Clauze suddenly stiffened. "Watch it. You can't make me do anything."

"I think I can," said Jouve.

"Don't be an asshole," said Clauze. "*I* paid my debt, too. I strayed, they found out, and they put me back to zero. I paid through the nose."

"You know damn well," Jouve pointed out, "that they never knew the half of it. You know I've kept the receipt."

So as to fill the heavy silence that followed, an automobile considerately drove up Avenue du Général Brunet.

"One day we'll settle this," Clauze said venomously.

"For sure," said Jouve. "One day we'll have to."

After another car had gone down the avenue in the opposite direction, Clauze finally stood up—I'll be back, I have to make a phone call—leaving behind his detective odor: essence of cafeteria and office, perfume of jail and slum, effluvium of hovel, oil of dump, everything a policeman passes through, everything a policeman must pass through. While awaiting his return, through the window Jouve watched the branch of a plane tree limply beat the air. Ten twenty-five.

Clauze reappeared with an appeased face, without apparent grievance, as if settling a perfectly normal matter, paper in hand and pride all swallowed. "Not easy to find," he said in a detached voice. "The guy I called at first thought she was dead, but I guess not. Anyway, we came up with this. You can give this a shot." Jouve glanced at the piece of paper: the address of a law firm near the Champs-Elysées.

"Thank you, Robert," he said. "I won't forget it."

"Fine," Clauze said calmly. "Now go to Hell."

At around eleven o'clock, Jouve returned to his office,

a former building manager's domain with very little light and a gray-painted window facing the street. He had kept the original furniture: tubes and latex, bottom of the line and not particularly comfortable. Not much better, in small business terms, than the police station of the Amérique quarter. Jouve read the paper and organized some files; Personnettaz appeared at noon sharp.

Personnettaz hadn't put on any weight. Unhealthy-looking as ever. Still that not-very-reassuring air of a soldier-monk. Jouve explained the situation: Kastner's disappearance, his replacement by Boccara, Gloire's personality. "She won't be easy," he said. "The kid can't handle it. What do you say to taking over?"

"I have some free time at the moment," Personnettaz uttered after a long silence. "In any case, I'll need an assistant."

"Take Boccara," Jouve offered. "He's young, but he'll make you a good little sidekick."

An hour later, in the lobby of Stochastic, Jouve's appearance clashed with the employees of that enterprise, and his teeth gnashed in their direction. He entered Salvador's office as the latter was going over the next episode of *The Prettiest Girl on the Beach* with Donatienne. "I've got this for you," said Jouve, holding out his brother-in-law's paper. "Excuse me, old friend," said Salvador, "but I'm a bit—you see." "I'm not your old friend," observed Jouve. "Beg your pardon?" said Salvador. "Oh, forgive me, Jouve, it's stress, I'm awfully sorry." ("OK," said Donatienne, "so there's a Mr. Yvon Querson who gave the name of a Miss Anabelle Fleury, who we found.") "No harm done," said Jouve. "Here." ("Who recognized herself," Donatienne continued, "who is now Mrs. Annabelle Schnitzler and who's agreed to come on the show.") "What *is* this thing?" Salvador grunted, glancing over the paper. "Hey, hold on, Jouve. Hey, wait a second. Hey, come back!" ("We'll have to notify the families," Donatienne projected, "and we've found some of her friends. We even found the lifeguard who was on duty that day at the beach.") "Shit," muttered Salvador, sitting back down in his chair after Jouve had gone, dignity ruffled, door left open behind him.

Salvador reread the paper that he'd stuffed in his pocket, tried to make heads or tails of it, then: "OK, that's fine —you can take care of that on your own. Let's get down to the important thing."

The tall blondes. Let's recapitulate. We'll proceed by auteurs. We have the Hitchcocks. Then we have the Bergmans. Then we have the ones from Soviet films, satellite nations included. After that we're not sure. Let's start over. Perhaps we'll proceed geographically instead. Mainly American, European, let's say from across the Atlantic to the Urals: tall blondes mostly populate the northern hemisphere. Yes. That's not a very good angle, either. We could begin with a classic reference, everyone included. Let's say the emblematic Monroe-Dietrich-Bardot triangle.

"Isn't that a little overdone?" wondered Donatienne. "Haven't we seen that a hundred times already?"

"Have it your way," said Salvador. "Fine. So we'll organize it by personalities. Let's forget the three classic tall blondes and turn to the oddities. Let's look at the special cases, like Anita Ekberg, you see, or Julie London in another genre. Hand me that file. Let's see. We have the solitary types, the marginals, the failures. We've also got a few insignificant ones. Plus we should mention a couple of comediennes. And take into account the very small number of ugly ones. How do we establish an order? How do we classify the whole thing?"

"Actually, she wasn't as tall as all that, Monroe," Donatienne observed, leaning over the file.

"Nothing to do with it," answered Salvador without raising his eyes, "you don't get my methodology. They don't absolutely need to be tall to fit into the category of 'tall blondes,' not necessarily." (He reflected.) "When you get down to it, maybe they don't even need to be blonde. I don't really know yet."

"Ah," went Donatienne, "forgive me. Forget I said anything. I guess I don't get it."

"My fault," said Salvador. "I'm just getting worked up. But maybe I'm getting off the track. Maybe I should make my criteria a little stricter. Honestly, what do you think? What do you think, deep down?"

CHAPTER 8

ANOTHER LATE AFTERNOON, almost evening. Gloire is sitting at the kitchen table, elbows on the waxed cloth, two fingers holding a cigarette whose end she taps more often than necessary against the rim of a Martell promotional ashtray. Today she isn't made up, except for her lips, saturated with a violent red that makes her face look even paler than usual. And re-dyed brown as planned, held back with a pink terrycloth loop, her hair is no better styled than last time.

She is not beautiful to behold, but fortunately there is no one there to behold her. Even so, why doesn't she fix herself up a little? She has her reasons, of course, but she could at least buy herself some new clothes once in a while, something a little more flattering, no?

No. She's wearing her sweater with its frosted bear cub pattern, and her feet are in dirty white and blue sneakers bearing the inscription *Winning Team*. Since it is not very warm in the kitchen—the only heat comes from a gas device with a reddening grill over which a brief tongue of magenta flame occasionally runs, producing a dull, vaguely frightening *whump* of air—Gloire has kept on her royal-blue ski parka, polyester and cotton with a polyamide lining, size 4.

It's now seven P.M. and she is alone again. Vexed, Beliard has left after yet another argument. The transistor radio still plays quietly on the table. Sometimes the young woman underscores three notes of a song in a low voice, sometimes she emits a kind of cluck that might make you think she's a little drunk. But no: into the mustard glass with Bugs Bunny's effigy sitting before her, Gloire has dipped her lips only once.

We can see little in that kitchen with its two anemic wall lamps and tube of neon over the sink. We can make out two folded, faded lawn chairs shoved into a corner, the cube-like refrigerator and greasy stove, the massive buffet table, the plastic flowered tablecloth, and two frames on the wall containing a photo of the Maréchal de Lattre and three sunflowers on canvas. The walls haven't been any particular color since the dawn of time and Gloire is sitting in the shadows, how bored she is tonight, oh my God tonight how bored can she be.

When they handed her the keys to the house, Gloire didn't change a thing, preferring not to impose any of her own tastes, which she abandoned. On the contrary, it was herself, her own person that she tried to make conform to the house, letting herself be impregnated, remodeled by this small, poorly lit, badly heated lodging, in a village of ninety-five souls squeezed between an arm of the sea and acres of cereal. Instead of replacing that tablecloth and turning the Maréchal de Lattre against the wall, it was the tablecloth and the photo that she let turn and replace what they wished in her. Rather than repaint the kitchen, Gloire asked the kitchen to choose the color of her blush and eyeliner, dictate her choice of clothes, words, and inflections, define the angle of her stoop.

Gloire Abgrall's life might not seem very happy, but that's the way she wants it. In the four years since she decided to disappear, erase herself from the face of the world and go underground, she has performed all her actions with this in mind, trusting her instincts. She cut all past ties, changed her name for the second time, to Christine Fabrègue, and transformed her appearance as we have seen. She has kept relations with her neighbors to a minimum, the only one allowed to converse with her being Alain. And in fact, there's a knock on the door and here he is. "Well, well," she thinks, "shithead's right on time."

So Alain enters, still wearing the same pullover—only, the temperature having dropped, a triangle of brown wool now emerges from the dip of the V. Stocky, condensed like a battery, electric-red hair; just add a socket and you could plug a lamp into him. Hesitant, he remains standing in the doorway, an uncertain smile floating over his lips. At the end of his arm dangles a live crab fat as a handbag. Berthaux has just given it to him, he explains, he himself doesn't know what to do with it, would Christine like it?

At first Gloire doesn't answer, distrustfully eyeing the tannish creature whose right front claw, bulkier than the left, convulsively pinches and releases the void, emitting signs. "Something to drink, Alain?" she says with some delay, after the crab is installed in the sink and has begun producing tiny bubbles of drool. About as mobile as a vaguely free-willed pebble, as a man fallen in his armor and trying to stand, the crab labors in vain to climb out of the sink. Moving in clumsy lateral jerks, it skids against the smooth sides and falls back onto its flank, secreting its fluid with the noise of a soggy mineral.

After sitting down, the ex-sailor resumes the tale of his maritime memories: expeditions, voyages, and injuries

that might add up to a full life. He has always been a
sailor: navy, merchant marine, fishing. He returns to his
impressions of Australia, the country that seems to have
left the deepest impression on him. Still, he's lacking his
usual verve: he pauses, sends expectant looks Gloire's way,
no doubt waiting for the young woman to address him
familiarly like the other day.

When Gloire gets up after a while to fetch some more
ice cubes, Alain's fuzzy gaze follows her toward the refrigerator. He stands in turn and walks up behind her as she's
foraging in the freezer. "You know I really like you,
Christine," Alain declares in a strangled voice. Gloire does
not answer immediately.

"It's important for neighbors to like each other," the
man frantically continues, "it's good to really like each
other. How can I put it—it's better."

The young woman turns around slowly, a wide mask-
like smile on her lips, in her hand two ice cubes that burn
her palm. "What are you saying?" she asks.

"Nothing bad about doing something good," the man
stammers, happy to see this smile, "that's what I meant."

"What are you going on about?" Gloire repeats softly
while walking toward Alain, who is ready to beat a retreat
and suddenly grows worried. But too late. Grabbing the collar of his V-neck with her free hand, Gloire pulls him close
and kisses him roughly, for two or three long seconds, before
violently pushing him away. "Get lost," she says. "Get out of
here now." As Alain tries to pull her back by one arm, Gloire
wrenches free before bringing her ice-filled hand down on
his face. A sharp corner of one of the cubes scrapes the forehead of the ex-sailor, who lurches back, lifting a hand to his
face and staring at the short smear of blood on his fingers.
Then scarcely has he raised his eyes back to Gloire than she
rushes forward, shoving him with punches and kicks toward

the door, and this man who has stood up to life's hardships, the fury of nature, physical confrontations, and adversity recoils before this unexpected force that pursues him even beyond the door, which is then slammed shut behind him. He flees down the road, toward his home, still without paying attention to the Volvo 360 parked in the same place as the day before, while Gloire, beside herself, goes to find a hatchet in the storeroom.

Back from the storeroom, tearing through the kitchen in a sweat, she spots the crab at the bottom of the sink. Spinning around, she hacks it in two with a single blow of the hatchet. And as she rushes toward the door, the animal's two halves continue to wave feebly each on its own side, in the mad hope of pulling closer and resoldering themselves, leaking shreds of transparent flesh.

Gloire reopens the door, bursts onto the threshold, tries to make out in the darkness the silhouette of Alain, who hasn't waited around for her. In both directions, the street is deserted. The only unfamiliar object is the Volvo 360 parked not far from the house, apparently empty, on which Gloire's gaze rests for a moment, and from which that gaze would immediately have come away if it hadn't been for the intermittent glow of a Pall Mall behind the fogged windows. *There they are again, back to get on my fucking tits.* The young woman's eyes narrow an instant before she begins walking with determined steps toward the car.

From inside that car, Boccara sees her approaching. Hatchet in hand, face of a Medusa, in the shadows she appears to surge from a barbarous pantheon, a Symbolist painting, or a horror film. She moves much faster than the mental processes of Boccara, who at first doesn't have the slightest reaction. By the time he finally moves his hand toward the ignition key, the hatchet crashes down onto the windshield which explodes just as the engine turns over.

In a deformed voice, Boccara emits an inarticulate cry of terror, hastily shifts into first as he stomps on the gas pedal. Gloire jumps away in time. After two clumsy swerves, the Volvo finds the direction of the road and disappears with its lights off. Not until five hundred yards later does Boccara remember to switch them on. The cold air rushes in through the absent windshield, cauterizing the little cuts on his face caused by shards of safety glass. Still, lucky for him he didn't take his chances by the cliffs: no doubt he would have fared much worse. But Gloire knows no means of cleansing the world other than the void.

CHAPTER 9

OVER THE FOLLOWING MILES, while shielding his eyes from the cutting night air and posing the pad of a cautious middle finger on his fresh wounds, Boccara hurled numerous loud imprecations against Gloire. Worried, dissatisfied, contracting his jaws, aching from his wounds whose gravity he hadn't assessed, Boccara demonstrated a fair amount of invention in his volley of invectives.

Forced to drive at a reduced speed, he also took a fair amount of time to reach Saint-Brieuc. At the city's entrance a service station was open, its functions diversified enough for them to handle his windshield problem. While they attached a temporary plastic film in its place, Boccara headed for the toilets to assess the damage—four or five very superficial cuts, nothing serious. He examined himself in the mirror: still the same young fellow, a bit chubby but with the eyes of a pretty girl, an alert air, not short enough to be short, not fat enough to be fat, not yet thin enough on top to be truly bald, but all that would happen soon enough. All that would surely happen, and so it bothered him. No matter what he did, in twenty years his future was settled: lotions and wedge heels, diet pills, jogging—nothing would help.

Still, he tried to smile almost all the time. Even in that moment of defeat before the mirror, alone in the gas station bathroom, batting his eyelashes, looking like he could let the world go for a song, he forced out his lighthearted smile, dusted with insouciance and topped with nonchalance. He brushed off the lapels of his beautiful prussian-blue jacket with its violet sheen. Always well dressed, Boccara chose his garments with care, from inside which he observed with troubled eye the mediocrity of the world, and of others' clothes in particular.

He headed back to the service station, settled the bill and asked for a receipt, then drove off. On the road back, the landscape as filtered through the plastic film was hazy, as if in a heavy fog, its motions jerky as in an old television. Prevented from driving at his usual speed, Boccara bore his cross patiently. Stretching out his lumbars, draping his forearms over the wheel, he enjoined himself to stay calm even though irritated by that slowness, by the hypocrisy of that slowness, majordomo of death, that feigned to ignore the brevity of existence.

Twenty miles back, Gloire also forced herself to calm down. After smashing the windshield and watching the Volvo flee, she took refuge inside her house, door double-bolted and shutters latched. Then she secluded herself with a glass of wine in the windowless bathroom, closing the door behind her, switching on the fluorescent light above the sink. The light, like the rest of us, had a hard time waking up; coughing and spitting up a little glimmer, it sputtered for a few seconds before glowing its entire length. Having lowered the toilet lid, Gloire sat down on top, chest forward, head dangling between her elbows which rested on her thighs, her hands joined in front of her around her glass. What's the situation?

Apparently they've found her. Located her, recognized her, followed her. Not only does Gloire have not the slightest idea as to the identities or intentions of the men who have tracked her down, but not the slightest curiosity either; for her, the only question is how to get rid of them. In the long term, any overt resistance seems vain: making Jean-Claude Kastner disappear has proven useless, and scaring off tonight's intruder will surely serve no purpose either. They seem to be well organized. They are obstinate. There might be many of them. They will be back. Despite all the care she has taken, the young woman's retreat now appears compromised. No more anonymity, no more peace, no more prolonged social coma. These men on her tail represent a rejected past, but one that has just surged up from the depths of time, propelled by a fat rubber band. Others in a similar situation might try to come to an understanding, negotiate with these men, get information about their plans, and then act accordingly. Others, perhaps, but not Gloire. The idea does not even occur to her.

She thought she had been there for only a moment, sitting under her neon, when an early bird began to moan and stretch, yawn while opening a first eye in the palm tree. Back in her room, four filaments of dark gray daylight already delineate the frame of the shutters. Then another moment later, lying fully dressed under a blanket, her eyes remain staring into the darkness. The sun as it rises finds her in a canvas chair in the middle of the garden, under the same blanket. Beliard appears at around nine thirty.

Beliard looks beat. Hasn't shaved or changed since the day before. Although preoccupied with other worries, Gloire has to restrain herself from asking where he spent the night; besides, he never tells. He seems not very talkative in any case, ill disposed to conversation. One might suspect him of having come just to get some rest, to doze peacefully nestled on the young woman's warm and supple shoulder. As the latter tries after a moment to bring him up to date on the night's events, the homunculus at first answers only in pouty, sometimes sarcastic, generally dismissive monosyllables. It seems that today isn't the day.

Today isn't the first time Beliard looks out of sorts, ignorant of what's been going on and its import. But it's always like this: sometimes he knows everything that has happened in his absence, even mentioning details that Gloire doesn't know, and sometimes he turns up aware of nothing, looking dazed, like this morning, and she has to explain everything to him—of course, it's also possible that Beliard might be faking it. Gloire shakes her shoulder to rouse him a bit.

"Listen to me, at least," she says. "It can't go on like this."

"What can't," grouses Beliard. "A lot of things can't go on like this."

"They were back again," says Gloire. "Another one, last night."

"Yeah, yeah," goes Beliard, barely sitting up, with a more or less informed smack of his pasty lips. "So?"

"I want them to leave me alone!" cries Gloire. "It's only going to get worse, don't you see? I thought it would be over after that guy the other night, but no, there are others and it's all going to start again. I don't want them to start pestering me again. Can't you understand that?"

"Fine," says Beliard, "fine. Calm down."

Then she plunges her face between her hands: "I just want everyone to leave me the fuck alone," she says again, but in a different tone, in a voice like the downward spiraling of a parachute.

She sobs for two or three minutes, while Beliard

mechanically pats her on the shoulder, throwing worried glances all around for fear the woman's cries have attracted attention. "Let's think about it," he says. "We'll find a solution."

"I've thought about it," she finally breathes into her hands.

"What have you thought about?" says Beliard, but she shrugs her shoulders without answering. "What have you thought about?" the homunculus insists.

"Nothing," she says after a moment. "And anyway, I can't."

She has blown her nose. She speaks in that voice of desperate, disillusioned anger that certain little girls in tears have, brave but jaded. "Anyway," she repeats, "it's not even possible."

"All right," says Beliard, "what's not possible?"

That she doesn't answer immediately might mean she doesn't dare. In spite of the fact that she treats Beliard rudely, that she often complains of his presence and wishes for his departure, it seems that Gloire always needs his opinion, his consent even his encouragement. At first, Gloire is afraid this opinion might be negative; then she finds that dependency humiliating. Finally: "I want to go away," she says softly. "I'd like to go away."

Beliard maintains a clinical silence.

"I'd really like to leave here," Gloire repeats, raising her head. "But no way, huh?"

More silence, then: "Well, why not?" Beliard says calmly. "It should be doable. I don't see any obstacles."

"You think?"

"Of course," Beliard repeats, "of course. Personally, I don't see any reason you couldn't."

Gloire looks skeptically at the homunculus, who continues: "Not only is it possible," he progressively warms up, "it might even be desirable. You've paid your dues, that's enough. You've done enough. It's all right. You can go. Here's what you do: you cash in your holdings and then skip off to the tropics, far away."

"No," says Gloire, incredulous.

"Yes," says Beliard, "yes, since I said so."

"All right," Gloire says cautiously after a brief pause. "All right, I'll do it your way. That's what you said, right? The tropics, far away?"

"That's exactly right," says Beliard. "And I'm coming with you."

"Hold on there," Gloire perks up, "hold on a moment. I can go perfectly well by myself."

"You're out of your mind," says Beliard. "Here's to the good life."

CHAPTER 10

"IN OTHER WORDS, SHE'S OUT OF HER MIND," concluded Boccara, cautiously fingering the gauze confetti scattered over his little wounds.

"In any case," said Jouve, "she seems to know how to handle herself."

"That's right, make jokes," Boccara objected. "How long will these things take to heal?"

"No time at all," said Jouve. "Three days, tops. Tell people you cut yourself shaving. What do you make of all this, Personnettaz?"

From his adjacent stool, Boccara cast an apprehensive eye at Personnettaz, who was rigidly seated in the armchair facing Jouve's desk: a thin, reclusive individual, austere though oddly costumed as a whimsical insurance agent, in a sand-colored suit and chocolate-brown shirt with light-green tie. Coppery, almost red hair in a military cut, sunken cheeks, and lined forehead; two long wrinkles parallel to the jawline could have passed for gashes or initiatory scarifications, and his icy stare gave Boccara the creeps. His face reflected a major preoccupation, or perhaps a great moral suffering, or maybe a chronic illness—an ulcer or something of the sort. He was attentive and serious as if at the doctor's. He had said nothing until then.

"It doesn't seem like much at first glance," he finally uttered without moving his lips.

"You're joking," said Boccara. "She's dangerous. She's completely gonzo."

"It didn't seem like much to me, either," said Jouve, "I know. At first I didn't even want to bother you. But now there's that Kastner business that's got me worried. Almost a week without a word; it's aggravating. I want to know what happened. I hope she didn't hurt him—I *am* his employer, after all. Now it's not only for the client's benefit that we need to find her. So how about it, then? Will you do it?"

"You know how I work," said Personnettaz. "I don't do anything without an assistant. And I've lost my assistant. I'm looking for another one."

"Well, take Boccara," suggested Jouve, "there's nothing he'd like better. He's very good."

"Sure!" exclaimed Boccara, "choose Boccara. Top quality, no defects. Don't think twice before saying OK!"

Personnettaz gave him the same grim look that he gave all things, the technical and disaffected gaze of someone judging distance on a rifle range. "Fine," he said, glancing at his iron wristwatch, "we'll try it. We leave in three hours. Before that I have to stop at my place."

Shortly afterward he walked across Boulevard des Batignolles, up the fraction of Rue de Rome that borders and overhangs the train tracks flowing into the Gare Saint-Lazare. Below the street ran some twenty parallel rails that the tall buildings overlooked in a sheer drop and on which trains passed from time to time. Riveted here and there to the protective fence, enameled plaques warned people not to touch the electric wires (mortal danger) or throw garbage onto the tracks.

Leaving the sidewalk of Rue de Rome, Personnettaz turned right onto the Pont Legendre, suspended over the tracks for thirty yards by a structure of cast-iron latticework. As he reached the middle of the bridge, the little convoy of four silvery wagons that linked Rouen with Paris appeared: seemingly made of tin plate, they ran over their rails following a northwest-southeast axis. Since Personnettaz, for his part, was following the bridge on a southwest-northeast axis, the paths of man and train intersected at a right angle, and for the space of one one-hundredth of a second his body was superimposed over that of the woman, inside the train, whom he had just agreed to find.

After her conversation with Beliard, Gloire had quickly organized her departure. She made a list of things to do. Housecleaning and straightening up in the morning, disposal of crab remains and putting to death of the rabbit. In the afternoon, gathering of her clothes and effects, which she had at first tried to sort before shoving them all into a polyeurethane bag that she immediately deposited by the door, in the spot reserved for trash. Drafting of a note for the landlord, which she would mail accompanied by a check and the two sets of keys. Purchase of a bottle of cognac. Preparation of rabbit marengo.

Early the following morning, she had taken the first train for Rouen, then the bus to a rest home located in a former convent on the outskirts of Rouen. After a short wait at the end of a corridor, a well-dressed old man, bright as a button, had shuffled up on the arm of a nurse. Gloire had kissed him. "Miss," the old man had said, "you are absolutely charming, but I don't believe we've been properly introduced." The nurse in the background shook her head.

"Here, Daddy," Gloire had said, "I've brought you some cognac." The nurse in the background shook her head in the other direction.

"You are infinitely kind," the old man lit up, "but I fear they might well confiscate it."

Then she had returned to the station and taken the second train toward Paris, Gare Saint-Lazare. She was coming back now. She was going home.

She had kept her miserable appearance and, despite the first-class ticket, retained her fourth-class clothes. Her travel bag was nearly empty, containing only a healthy sum of money in five-hundred-franc bills, which she went to count once in the train lavatory. She studied herself in the mirror, shoulders hunched forward, face stubborn. That was sufficient now; she had seen herself that way long enough—but soon it would be the end of that look. Patience, old girl.

At the Gare Saint-Lazare, as she passed into the field of the surveillance cameras, she noticed once again her poor silhouette, full-length this time, on the monitors mounted above the information boards: it had been a while since she'd seen herself onscreen. Gloire hadn't watched herself often, in any case, in the short time of her instant celebrity, which had set like a sun after having barely risen. On television it had first been three or four variety shows that were never rebroadcast, just enough time to lip-sync "Excessive" followed by "We're Not Taking Off," then immediately afterward, during the trial, a few brief appearances at the end of the news, always in the Celebrity or Crime updates. After that she had never again appeared on a TV screen. Had never seen herself on one again except in the household appliance sections of department stores, on the screens of video equipment being demonstrated for private individuals or, just before her departure from Paris, on the monitors that show the platform comings and goings of similar private individuals to the Metro conductors.

But from now on, Gloire would avoid the Metro. A taxi brought her to a small, quiet hotel on a small, quiet street on the fringes of Montparnasse. The hotel didn't look like a hotel but, instead, like something halfway between a family pension and a trysting place. No reception desk to speak of, only a living room in which a discreet and distinguished woman, tailored suit and pearl necklace, handed her a key with no questions asked—no numbers on the room doors, either. Gloire set down her bag and immediately went back out, then headed up Rue de Rennes on foot.

Near Sèvres-Babylone, three or four afternoon hours would suffice for her to reconstitute a wardrobe without worrying about the cost: a raincoat and two skirts, two pairs of trousers, four permanent-press pleated skirts made in Japan, two similar pairs of rope sandals with platform heels. Then, passing by Guerlain, she went in to buy herself a few light products, almost no makeup, tonic and cleansing lotion, a small atomizer of Jardins de Bagatelle. On Rue de Grenelle, finally, Gloire bought two expensive leather handbags in which to stuff her new acquisitions.

After she returned to the hotel to change, barely made up, a second taxi dropped her in the ministerial quarter, in front of a low, elegant building with no sign to indicate its business. Two globes of shrubbery framed a door of translucent glass and wrought iron. Once she had slipped into a white robe on the ground floor and climbed a flight of stairs, the man one floor up made a concerned face when he saw her coming but evinced no surprise; he would ask no questions. "It's me," said Gloire.

"Of course," said the man. "So I see."

Comb-name: Caesar—a large pensive bird with metal-rimmed glasses and the shaved head of an atomic scientist. He pointed her toward a chair. "Do sit down," he said. "I'm delighted to see you again. May I offer you some coffee?"

She took her place before a mirror and Caesar, without uttering the slightest commentary, passed three fingers through her hair, lifting a lock, thoughtfully gauging another and reserving his diagnosis. "Dear me," he finally said in a distressed tone. "It wasn't you who cut this last time, was it?" Gloire nodded, smiling. "I see," went Caesar. "So? Do I try to make the best of what's here, or do I take it all from scratch?"

"All from scratch," said Gloire, "just the way it was. The same color as before."

He stood behind her, looked her in the eye in the mirror, having placed his hands delicately on her shoulders. "How long has it been," he asked gently, "three years?"

"Four," said Gloire.

Those eyes bathed her in an affectionate gaze that was dismantled, then discreetly rebuilt into a sarcastic one. "You haven't changed a bit," he said. "I don't mean your hair, of course." He reached for his scissors.

An hour and a half later, the sun was about to set when Gloire crossed the Seine via Pont de la Concorde and walked up the Champs-Elysées. The light was silky and blonde, and so was Gloire. She had regained the status of tall blonde; she stood straight; she hardly seemed crazy at all. Once again men turned their heads as she passed by.

On Rue de Tilsitt, between the Belgian embassy and the Zimbabwean embassy, the offices of Bardo, attorneys at law, occupied an entire second floor. Brown carpeting and abstract art in the reception area. Having asked to see Mr. Lagrange, Gloire waited a few minutes, alone in a room huge enough to produce an echo. A very nervous young lawyer appeared, short and austere as a printed form, who soberly requested that Gloire follow him to the padded door of his office, but who, once the latter was shut, began dancing frenetically around the young woman, throwing his head back and beating the air with his arms, all the while exclaiming that it had been so long, that he was so happy, that she hadn't changed a bit. Gloire smiled: people's opinions concurred.

Lagrange calmed down progressively, the way a superball gradually stops bouncing, before sitting back at his desk where, for a few minutes more, he continued to bobble on his chair. Even after he had settled down, Lagrange remained an essentially feverish man, mounted like Donatienne on supercharged batteries and swarming with facial tics; under the effect of this agitation, his small man-tailored suits wore out more quickly on him than they would on others. Four or five times, six years earlier, Gloire recalled having shared his bed: all night long he was everywhere at once. He was basically a lawyer without a cause and was not especially looking for one, having enough money behind him to take on only risky cases and still drive an Opel. But honest. With Gloire, at least. It was to him that had befallen the task of managing the young woman's assets and overseeing her interests, free of charge. "My little Gloire," he said, "I'm here, you know I'm here. I Am Here." He had known her since childhood, or just about; he was more or less the only one aware of the entire situation. Unlike Caesar, he asked a lot of questions. Gloire was free to answer as she wished. But for the moment, what she mostly wished was to go away.

"Where?" asked Lagrange.

"As far away as possible," she said.

"As far away as possible," Lagrange repeated dreamily. "Apart from New Zealand, or Australia, I don't really see…"

In Gloire's mind, in fast motion, Alain's Australian adventures suddenly paraded by. Fauna, flora, aborigines, pearl divers; steaks with jelly and primitive minds. "Fine," she said, "let's say Australia."

"You sure you're sure?" worried Lagrange.

"Yes," said Gloire, "and I'd also like some new identity papers. Find me another name."

"Money first," said the lawyer, pulling various bank records from Gloire's file. It emerged from his perusal, first, that spread out over stocks, bonds, and rental units, the fortune at Gloire's disposal was rather sizeable. And second, that this capital had considerably accumulated lately, as the monthly checks Lagrange sent to Brittany were well below the interest earned by these investments. Perfect. To which Gloire responded, first, that she would be needing much larger sums during this trip. And second, that no, there was nothing new in her life, in particular no new man; she simply felt like getting away. She refrained from mentioning Kastner's visit and its sequel. Perfect.

Then they examined the Australian future. Lagrange would take care of everything: airplane tickets, visas, wire transfers, reservations, General Delivery. "And don't forget my name," Gloire reminded him, "and my papers."

"Fine," said Lagrange. "It might be a bit complicated, but I'll manage. What kind of name would you prefer?"

"Whatever you like," said Gloire. "You choose."

"Fine," said Lagrange. "Can I take you to dinner?"

As Beliard had not shown his face that entire day, Gloire felt more inclined after dinner to down a drink and then another drink and then a final drink with Lagrange, and then, one thing leading to another, the sperm of Lagrange, but she returned to her hotel fairly early and went to bed quickly, imagining the other end of the world. Envisioning at the other end of this vile world an undiscoverable, inviolable, unreachable retreat. A marsupial's pouch in which to snuggle, and then hop, hop, ever farther toward a better horizon to forget even her own name, all her names.

CHAPTER 11

IT WOULD BE NOTHING LIKE THAT. Gloire would see no kangaroos, koalas, or anything. Just one evening, in a gutter on Exhibition Street, she would notice the remains of an opossum lying between the front fender of a Holden Commodore and the rear fender of a Holden Apollo.

She had taken the Paris-Sydney flight via Singapore and Jakarta, which then continues on to Nouméa. In this airplane, freed from their military duties, twenty New Caledonian conscripts were heading home. *So long,* damp barracks; *so long,* nasty climate: the young men abundantly celebrated their discharge with shouts, libations, speeches, and songs. Once returned to civilian life, they had swapped their military effects for more whimsical uniforms of Rastafarian inspiration: stripes and shoulder braids for pendants and badges depicting Africa, a cannabis leaf, or Peter Tosh; khaki forage caps for ample woolen bonnets shaped like twenty-four-egg omelettes, hand-woven in green-yellow-red tricolor. The joy of seeing their native country again sometimes translated into a few minor exactions. Thus, when the beverage cart paraded by, pushed by a stewardess, it was with one hand that they snatched up a whole raft of burgundy and bordeaux, then, once the cart had passed, with the other that they affectionately smacked the rear end of the stewardess, who stiffened slightly under the impact, then turned around with a constrained smile. "Easy, easy," the two noncommissioned officers charged with bookending them then intervened, debonnaire. "Take it easy, guys."

One of the NCO's happened to be sitting next to Gloire. Native of Wallis and Futuna, he was a massive top sergeant who overflowed his seat when asleep, but who, when awake, made a little conversation with her. Placid smile and bull neck, a drinker of water, the top sergeant had taken part in all the national military expeditions of the last twenty years: from Comoro to Lebanon, from Niger to Gabon, from the Persian Gulf to the Red Sea. From his operations in Chad he kept a mixed impression, each mission having required him to back a different side. The other NCO, whom Gloire liked immediately, was a tall, handsome black with soulful eyes whom the top sergeant introduced as a heavyweight boxer for the French army. A great hope in his category. So Gloire addressed him a look full of hope. The transfer of the dismissed back to hearth and home required such heavy-duty measures, the sergeant explained, without which, left to their own drunken devices, they never failed to cause diplomatic incidents at the stopovers.

Then it was time for the meal trays. Gloire ate what they gave her, drank what she wanted, even after the lights went out and the movie began. The passengers had screwed their headphones into their ears, except for Gloire and a few others who, with no other soundtrack than the engines, distractedly leafed through magazines on their knees. Two hours later, everyone was asleep; even the conscripts had settled down. Discreetly, Gloire stood up to go to the lavatory, casting on the way a sober but precise glance at the handsome heavyweight from the French army, who joined her there twenty seconds later and kept her company for twenty minutes. Later, in Singapore, she visited only the duty-free shops in the airport, while locals dressed in apple green disinfected the Boeing; then, at the stopover in Jakarta, a sleeping Gloire saw nothing at all.

Time is always approximate on long-distance flights; one never knows exactly where one is among the various time zones. On the other hand, near Porte Dorée it was five P.M. sharp when Jouve, returning from the address indicated by his brother-in-law, stopped in to see Salvador. The latter paid scant attention, preoccupied as he was with a central theme (warm tall blondes versus cool tall blondes) of his project.

"A fellow named Lagrange," said Jouve. "He didn't want to tell me anything, claims he doesn't know her; he tried to pull the professional confidence routine, that whole business. But I'm sure he knows something. I think I'll try going about it a different way."

But Salvador, eager to see Jouve out: "Very good," he said, "do as you think best." Jouve gone: "Take this down," he said to Donatienne. "Here we go."

Certain incandescent tall blondes rush forward into the world with open arms. They speak vivaciously, laugh freely, think quickly, and drink heartily. They look proudly at the world, toss it terrible and generous smiles. Sometimes the world becomes flustered at the sight of them, sometimes it is intimidated by that sure, confident, low-necked way they have of rushing toward it, toward you, arms wide open in the direction of your own. The gaiety, the fearsome gaiety of those solar tall blondes.

"You might note Kim Novak in the margin, for example. What photos do we have of Kim Novak?"

They owned several stills of the bell tower scene in *Vertigo*, among them a vertical shot of the staircase (combination of tracking out and forward zoom), but Salvador is himself very prone to vertigo, so prone that even the slightest image of a steep plunge makes him nauseous. "No," he said, "find something else. That's enough for today."

"Right," said Donatienne. "And what about the cool ones?"

"How's that?" said Salvador.

"The cool tall blondes," she specified. "For the moment, you've only talked about the warm ones."

"We'll get to them later," said Salvador. "Can't do everything at once."

A little later, having reached her destination, Gloire settled into a hotel near Darling Harbour where, via a telex from Lagrange, a room had been reserved for her with a balcony overlooking the bay of Port Jackson. To counter the unease of the time change, she had first slept fifteen straight hours, then, on awakening, had made herself comfortable on the balcony, spending the majority of her time there in a deck chair in the company of Beliard.

The latter, who had not been around since Gloire's transformation, had reappeared the moment she found herself alone in her room. Inspecting her from head to toe: "Ah," he'd exclaimed, "I must say I like you better like this." Those first days, in short-sleeved shirt and Bermuda shorts, lying full-length across the footrest of the deck chair, the homunculus seemed to be in tip-top form. Wearing sunglasses made to his size, he trimmed his nails while whistling, gazing at the bay crisscrossed by fat, dark, ramshackle metallic ferries, and sunbathed in maximum-protection sunscreen.

For the Aussie sun is not like other suns: it burns you before you've even gotten warm, a vengeful blowtorch even in cool weather. And its path is not typical, either: jumping up in the morning, carbonizing everything in its rapid wake, it rushes to set at the precise moment in ten minutes flat, without dusk or any sort of protocol, and then night falls like a stone. Refreshing the cool drinks, the bellboys cautioned Gloire against it, advised her to protect herself, adjusted the opening of her parasol. She seldom went out. Everything was just fine.

And yet, less than a week after their arrival, it seemed that Beliard was starting to get restless. His mood seemed to have changed. He scarcely answered when Gloire talked to him, gave his opinion of the weather less frequently. Then one afternoon, when he opened his mouth, it was to posit that he was getting a bit fed up with that goddam sun and to suggest they go out for a walk, that they forget about this goddam balcony for a while. "All right," said Gloire. But outside, the sun was just as much of an issue. As Beliard was still invisible to the eyes of common mortals, he and Gloire had hardly gone a hundred yards toward the harbor when they collapsed into the first deck chair and under the first umbrella they found, annexes to a milkshake parlor. After a moment, Gloire had dozed off. When she opened her eyes again, Beliard was nowhere to be found: it seemed he had taken advantage of the open air and the young woman's nap to slip away. As if he needed that, she puzzled as she returned to the hotel. Thus, it was all alone that she would spend the following days.

CHAPTER 12

"BLESS YOU, GILBERT," said Personnettaz.

"I think I'm catching cold," Boccara observed, pinching his sinuses.

"We're wasting a ton of time," noted Personnettaz. "This is annoying."

"Jesus Christ, this thing is tight!" cried Boccara. "It looks like it's totally stuck."

Personnettaz's only response was to grimace one more notch, shrugging a shoulder already practically dislocated by the effort. Boccara pushed down on the crank as hard as he could, but the nuts seemed welded to the threads, riveted to the shanks. The fine, cold rain mixed with his tepid sweat in a warm, salty cocktail that blurred his vision, running over his eyes toward his lips: everything was conspiring against his attempts to change that right rear tire.

Crank in hand, Boccara was kneeling before his flat, whose rim spewed out some flaccid sections of wall. His palms, darkened by engine grease the moment he had grabbed the jack, now sprouted a few blisters as well. With all his weight, the young man bore down on the tool, standing up from time to time to try to unstick the whole mess with huge kicks, in vain: detaching itself from the bolt, the crank then rebounded noisily into the landscape where Boccara went to fetch it while cursing, scattering the accessories lying around him.

He and Personnettaz were on the shoulder of a six-lane highway—two times three separated by a divider sown with comatose plants and bordered by tumescent guardrails—cut off from the rest of the world by a fence between whose links danced scraps of plastic, fabric, and dirty, crumpled papers agglutinated at the feet of the road signs. Beyond this frontier, the world couldn't decide between fallow field and construction site. Not a single walking human to be seen.

Earlier than usual, under an iron sky, drivers in the fast lane had turned on their headlights, whose beams dimmed the daylight still further. Meowings of the vehicles and hissing of their tires on the slippery surface, intermittent gusts of wind and shivers down the spine. It was Tuesday, ten minutes before noon.

Standing behind Boccara, holding a light retractable umbrella, Personnettaz struggled to shelter the young man and himself—a task compromised by the insufficient diameter of the umbrella, which was shaken by the squall and occasionally upturned, and most often protected nothing more than a small uncertain zone between them, while they got soaked.

"You want me to try?" Personnettaz offered now and then.

"Skip it," went Boccara.

Unless a sensitive soul lent them a strong hand, their combined efforts must have succeeded, for two hours later they were back on the road, headlights on bright as they raced down the left-hand lane. Boccara's fingers left black-ish traces all over the interior, hardly noticeable on the seats and wheel but very distinct on his shirt collar, his forehead, his eyelids, and the wings of his nose, which were lighter in hue.

Returning from their mission without having found anything but Gloire's deserted house, the two men were silent: Boccara was pouting; Personnettaz was never very talkative. They switched on the radio for the news, which was at the forecast segment. The person responsible for it contented himself with quantifying the lousy weather that was visible through the car windows. Apparently exposed on the front lines to the very storms he was describing, his hoarse, febrile voice guaranteed the sound-ness of his pronouncements.

Stiff with exhaustion, Boccara also shivered inside his rumpled suit. Bad taste in his mouth, as if he were emerg-ing, sticky and disheveled, from a long, sleepless night in midday. At first demoralized by the narrowness of the world, twenty miles outside Paris he tried to lift his spir-its. Even though Personnettaz scared the willies out of him, he lowered the volume on the radio, then—perhaps in an effort to exorcise his discomfort—"So how about girls?" he asked with a joyless smile. "Do you get many opportunities, in your work?"

But he refrained from going further. The other, immo-bile and mute as usual, stared fixedly in front of him with an air of annoyance, or worry, or suffering. In a very bad mood or simply desperate, hard to say. One could sense his negative thoughts without really being able to divine their content. Not daring to pursue the matter, Boccara thought he might try distracting him with a variation on the same theme. To pick up girls, for example, how did he, Boccara, go about it?

"Simple," he answered himself, "simple. I sit alone at an outdoor cafe, I order a beer, and I pull a long face. And it never fails. Inside of a half hour, there's always one who comes by and sits down. And off you go."

Without emitting the slightest commentary, Personnettaz shot him a rapid glance, a brief composite look in whose heart envy, skepticism, and reprobation glared at each other. Then he turned the radio back up: Shostakovich. Boccara didn't dwell on the subject. They listened to Shostakovich. He's not so bad, Shostakovich; some of his quartets are really very nice. Then once in Paris, near the Opera, Personnettaz had him stop the car in front of a telephone booth. "Wait for me here," he said, opening the door. "I'll report in to the client." At around two-something P.M., the sky had calmed down, the shops reopened. The neighborhood proved to be abundant in salesgirls returning from their low-calorie lunches, their liter-and-a-half of Evian under their arms: Boccara modified the tilt of his seat the more comfortably to watch them heading back to their work stations.

But Salvador, who had just had himself delivered a club sandwich and a beer in his office, was in no mood to answer when the phone rang. Before his eyes, the tall blondes file was open to the delicate point of artificial blondes. "Right," he said quickly, "yes, so it's a bust? How should I know? Ask Jouve." He hung up quickly so as not to lose his train of thought, trying to explore this point, thinking aloud. Taking dictation on the other side of the office, Donatienne simultaneously projected photos of Stéphane Audran, Angie Dickinson, and Monica Vitti on a wall screen to stimulate Salvador's reflections. The latter paused briefly, distracted by the telephone call. Then: "Every blonde, one day or another," he resumed, "faces the suspicion that she's a fake. Every one of them is exposed to this doubt; each one runs the risk they'll be suspected of being artificial. Now, the artificial blonde is sometimes more pertinent, more representative than the true one, what do you think?"

But today, Donatienne didn't feel like thinking, or even like talking at her usual speed.

"Depends," she said. "Can you expand on that?"

"I think so," said Salvador. "We'll come back to it. Let's move on. The artificial blonde is thus a specific category, a style apart. Which the artificial brunette isn't. In any case, the artificial brunette is improbable, we can't see any reason for her to exist. She doesn't create an event the way an artificial blonde can, who has chosen her color with this one objective in mind. So coloring your hair only scandalizes in one direction, you follow me?"

"Whatever you say," yawned Donatienne. "Go on."

"I saw one go by," Boccara announced when Personnettaz got back in the car. "You should have seen her teeth when she smiled, the way they shined. I've never seen such white teeth, I'm telling you, it was like a whole bathroom."

"Go on, drive," uttered Personnettaz.

"Sorry," said Boccara.

They headed via Saint-Lazare toward the Europe quarter, where the light often reminds one of Eastern Europe; where in streets more open than elsewhere, via more obtuse perspectives, an undercurrent of chilly air persists even in warm weather; where noises sound as if they were coming from a bit farther away. A few of those streets, the most introverted ones, retain a slight air of vacation or penury all year round: for example, in front of Jouve's office, there were loads of places to park.

Symmetrical to this office, another, larger office housed the headquarters of an association of women each more beautiful than the next. When Personnettaz and

Boccara entered the foyer, it appeared that a general assembly of this association was being held; Boccara poked his nose through the half-open door.

"Go on, move," said Personnettaz.

"Sorry," said Boccara.

Jouve was awaiting them for the debriefing. They informed him of their failure. "I'm not surprised," he said. "She's obviously cleared out. Anyway, too bad. We'll try something else. You'll need to go someplace, I'll explain where, but you'll have to do it rather discreetly, if you see what I…"

"Yes," said Personnettaz, "I see what you…"

A little later, furnished with Lagrange's address, they left the office while the general assembly of magnificent women was in full swing; in a riotous climate, they feverishly resolved to put matters to a vote.

"What now?" asked Boccara. "Are we going right away?"

"Why?" said Personnettaz. "Did you have something better to do?"

The same, a little later still, Rue de Tilsitt: "You want me to try?"

"Skip it," went Boccara.

Standing behind him now for some time, with flashlight in hand, Personnettaz endeavored to illuminate Boccara, who was completely absorbed in his task. He only partially succeeded. Under the effect of the prolonged immobility, his wrist occasionally weakened, causing the beam to veer toward an intermediary space between them, at which point they couldn't make out a thing. Boccara protested. Personnettaz raised the flashlight back up with two hands. It was ten minutes past twelve, already Wednesday.

Still fairly damp outside. On the tall windows of Lagrange's office, the increasingly fine rain, now almost fog, intermittently came to beat softly against the panes, the way gentle waves rumple sand. From Rue de Tilsitt rose a sporadic but sustained sound of traffic. Midnight at Place de l'Etoile: the more muffled halo of the surrounding boulevards farther on, ambulance siren here, car horn there. Nothing to do but listen to all that; nothing to see beyond the beam of the flashlight. Through the door leading to the office, a small glow from the streetlights weakly shone, barely accentuating the contours of the furniture without actually illuminating anything.

They had set up in the little annex to Lagrange's large office, a closed, windowless space of about fifty square feet. Fax machine and metal file cabinets, copy machine and sink, old-model safe: Boccara was kneeling on the carpet before the safe. Files were lying on this safe, from which a few onionskin sheets tried to escape. Sitting next to Boccara was a bag containing small tools, punches and pliers, feelers, a larger apparatus shaped like a suction cup, and a stethoscope. Sometimes Boccara donned the stethoscope, listened to the mechanism while counting the clicks, while trembling a bit—trembling sometimes to the point of botching a turn, having to start his calculations from zero, but also sweating at least as much as he was trembling; his moist fingers lost their hold on the slippery knob, and then there was that other guy behind him who lowered the flashlight just at the wrong moment: everything was conspiring against his attempts to open that safe.

The other one behind him, leaning over his shoulder, saw his assistant perspiring.

"You should have remembered to bring some rags," he said. "Are you sure you don't have any rags in your bag, there? You didn't bring any Kleenexes for your cold, did you?"

"No," Boccara huffed, "no, no, no. Goddammit, this

thing is slippery. I can't believe how hard it is to get a grip —Jesus!"

Interrupting his labors an instant to take a breather, he stifled a sneeze in the palm of his hand.

"Calm down," said Personnettaz. "You're wasting time."

"It feels like it's going into my chest," sniffled Boccara. "I can tell already. Then it'll be months before I can get rid of it. To hell with your blessings, Mr. Personnettaz."

CHAPTER 13

AFTER TAKING HIS FRENCH LEAVE, Beliard hadn't shown his face again. Gloire wasn't bothered that much by his absence, although sometimes she missed his conversation. Fair weather, in any case, over the entire South Pacific.

That Wednesday, day broke with its usual suddenness. After a rapid shower and a quick breakfast, the young woman quickly left her room. A cover for symphonic, well-trimmed rock orchestra sputtered affectionately in the elevator, and Gloire exited the hotel under the already harsh sun. She took the Pyrmont Bridge, for pedestrians only, up to the large aquarium. Then six hundred yards beyond rose a building in Anglo-antipodal style—luxurious shopping galleries all in lusters and balusters, copper and display windows, rugs, paintings, moldings—and facing it stood a pale marble statue of Queen Victoria. Gloire took the escalator to the top floor and sat at a low table glued to a varnished handrail beside a sheer drop, near a bridal boutique named Seventh Heaven. From there, her eye plummeted down three levels of art galleries, concessions of international couturiers, and dealers in luxury items, recent antiques, and heterogeneous souvenirs.

Once a bartender, sporting a Walkman, had brought her what she desired—coffee, ashtray—Gloire observed the traffic of fiancées who came and went around Seventh Heaven. Young or already not so young, the fiancées never came alone but always flanked by an attendant: mother, best friend, sister, or sister of the groom-to-be who was out there somewhere, drinking his last few beers with his oldest pals while waiting out the countdown. Installed on white leather loveseats, the attendants proffered or leafed through advice and catalogues. The fiancées seemed rather sure of themselves during the fittings. One could make out some belated hesitations on the faces of some, while the looks of others remained cold or else preoccupied with clandestine thoughts, and a few seemed embarrassed at not being able to hide their contentment; even though for the most part they weren't anything special, at least they'd managed to find someone. Through the shop window, Gloire watched them pose in their getups. Then, in mid-morning, as the boutique had emptied out, she entered.

Pale green or pale pink veils, deep purple and pearl rugs. Cylindrical satin-velvet display racks loaded with hats, necklaces, and shoes multiplied by large full-length mirrors with ornate frames. From among the hangers bearing processions of immaculate, frothy, effervescent gowns, Gloire chose a classic model, high-waisted, long, with lateral pleats, discreet scoop-neck whose obtuse angle would leave little more than her collar bones exposed. She shut herself up in the minuscule dressing room.

By magic she reemerged a quarter of a second later, encased in the gigantic outfit, followed by a squadron of salesgirls carrying far behind her several yards of train—the way a magician pulls out of his opera hat a dove fleeing a cat fleeing dogs followed by horses, camels, and ele-

phants that shuffle placidly toward the wings while bleat-
ing, meowing, trumpeting, and defecating along the way;
then by cohorts dressed in regional costumes who parade
while saluting the public under their applause, waving
hats and flags, announced by fanfares and trailed by village bands—and, all things considered, not very well fitted
out, spangled with tags, mounted all lopsided on white
high heels.

Gloire then let the salesgirls adapt the apparatus to her
body, adjust her waist, fix her shoulders, knot a tassel
around her groin, make a white lace hortensia blossom
between her breasts, dress her hair with a twist of ribbon
foliage, spread the veil over her face, adjust the cascades
of fabric, smooth out the wrinkles, insert pins in every
direction, and sign the whole thing with three rows of
pearls. That done, wedged into her gown, she attempted a
few careful movements, little precautionary reverences
addressed to her image, the single bride in the mirror.
"Well," she said, "I'll have to think about it."

Dressed again, Gloire spent the afternoon on one of
the ferries that join up with the circular dock in Manly,
then returned to her hotel; after dinner, since she didn't
feel like going to bed quite yet, the concierge gladly provided her with the address of a club in which she could
kill the rest of her night.

She easily found the establishment, frequented particularly by Westerners of the Northern Hemisphere, among
them a fair number of Westerners of the Northern
Hemisphere who were drunk, including a tall, thin Swiss
at the bar with a sad smile beneath his mustache. An organ-
ist could be heard in the background. Through the fog of
conversations, as if from behind a waterfall, the Hammond
organ discreetly inflected sticky sounds, nasal arguments
alternating with coughing fits and bellows blasts. The Swiss,

who dealt in environmental issues, offered Gloire a glass of local champagne; then they chatted, or more precisely the Swiss painted a somber portrait of Australia: more and more tourists on the ground, less and less ozone in the sky. He seemed to have his work cut out for him here.

Gloire had no sooner emptied her glass than the man immediately, without interrupting his soliloquy, had it refilled, several times. Gloire smiled, a lot of people smiled, the organ continued to talk through its nose, spreading its chords with marmalade or panting like a beast of burden. Just back from Labrador, the Swiss now discoursed on the fate of Labrador seals, mass-exterminated so that their pelts could be made into slippers and key holders, and especially into little jointed toys shaped like Labrador seals. Gloire herself was getting rather drunk and seeing the world through glass, all perceptions anaesthetized, like a blaze cooled by the television screen. When the glass began to cloud over, it was time to go home. The Swiss man was very nice, but no, not tonight; perhaps she'd come back tomorrow to see if he was still there. Gloire stood up carefully, thanked the man, and left the establishment.

The silence in the street, when she came out, was the kind one listens to like a sound. Relieved to see herself walking fairly straight, to clearly read two in the morning on her watch, Gloire preferred to walk home rather than take a taxi. The nightclub was located several blocks from the aquarium, beyond which, via the Pyrmont Bridge, she could get back to her hotel. Not too many people at this hour near the aquarium; not a soul on the Pyrmont Bridge.

But alas, actually there is: shortly after she sets foot on the bridge, a distant soul comes to set foot in the opposite direction. At first indistinct, gradually becoming sharper, this soul is about fifty years old, hefty and dressed in dark blue; male gender. The man advances at a leisurely pace

on Gloire's left, while she keeps to her right without raising her eyes. As they are about to cross paths, the man suddenly veers toward her and utters several words that she
does not understand. Never was very brilliant in foreign
languages, that Gloire. More or less able to manage in a
hotel porter's English, but completely unequal to holding
a conversation, especially at this hour, and given her present state and the Australian accent. As she shakes her
head—*don't speak English*—and quickens her step, the man
turns and begins following her, walking alongside while
repeating the same formula, this time in a more pressing
interrogative tone, and soon gripping her arm just above
the elbow. Gloire begins walking more quickly still, shaking her head—*leave me alone*—and trying to free herself
with a few icy looks. The man then grabs her by the shoulder, forcing her to stop, and spinning her toward him he
grabs her other shoulder.

Gloire tries to struggle, but the other holds her firmly,
pulling her toward his large, perspiring body as he edges
toward the retaining wall. And then Gloire's strength
abandons her; then she is too afraid even to cry out in that
place, which in any case is deserted; already nearly asphyx-
iated by the sweat and breath of this man who is emitting
hissed, enraged words. She is incapable of altering the
course of events. Everything seems lost when Beliard, out
of nowhere, suddenly rises from the young woman's shoulder and begins to yell, face contorted in hate. "Destroy the
bastard!" he screams. "Rip his balls off! Tear his mother-
fucking eyes out!"

Gloire will never know if the man noticed Beliard's war-
like presence. Whatever the case, for one instant he seems
confused, loses his balance, then more forcefully resumes
his grip, spitting at Gloire's face short, new words that she
can't understand, but of which she nonetheless gets the

gist. But such is Beliard's power that he regenerates cells, multiplies energy: immediately afterward, under the force of a new resistance, an unexpected counterattack, the man finds himself abruptly thrown to the ground and his head thuds dully against the pavement. He cries out, tries to get up. Perhaps he already intends to admit defeat; perhaps he'd let the matter drop with this woman and her tenfold strength if Beliard, stamping his feet on her shoulder, didn't keep exhorting Gloire, who jerks the aggressor upright. Without giving him a chance to run, she shoves him against the retaining wall and slaps him violently, many times over, and the man's look, which swings crazily between pain and astonishment, finally comes to rest on the young woman with an air of exhaustion, as if saying fine, OK, that's enough, you win.

The whole thing might have stopped there. Gloire would have ended up letting the man go if Beliard, up against her ear, weren't screeching at her to annihilate the piece of shit, rip him to shreds. So that in the wake of a final slap, she brusquely hooks the man's shoulder, twists his arm behind his back to the point of fracture, and turns him against the wall; then, grunting briefly like an animal, she knocks him with her shoulder over the guardrail and pushes him into the void. Dumbfounded, eyes open, the man falls without having understood anything about anything, so surprised that he doesn't even think to cry out. The waters of Port Jackson silently engulf him twenty yards below. All things considered, Beliard can certainly come in handy from time to time.

But twenty minutes later, after returning to her hotel still shaking with hatred, excitement, and fear, still pumped up by this energy, downing two whiskies one after the other—twenty minutes later everything turned around: Gloire collapsed in tears, prostrate on the edge of her bed, driven to despair by her irrepressible habit of throwing people from windows, cliffs, or bridges. Beliard, sitting nearby, stared thoughtfully at her. "There now, there now," he said in a consoling voice.

At first, Gloire was unable to utter a single word. Then: "Didn't have to do that," she sobbed, "we didn't have to do that."

"Skip it," said Beliard, "enough with the conscience. Sometimes you have to set an example. They'll never find out, in any case, but still we should probably think about going somewhere else. I'll do some checking into flights tomorrow. And as for you, you're going to get some sleep now, all right?"

"I can't," said the young woman.

"I'm not surprised," said the homunculus. "What have you got left in the way of pills?"

Gloire went to get her pouch of hypnotics, from among which Beliard mixed a potent cocktail, and a little while later everything was calm and the woman was asleep, finally seeming at peace; the little blue veins on her temples throbbed tranquilly. Far from the world she floated: perhaps nothing had happened at all.

But the next morning, when the wake-up call came a bit too early, there was no longer the slightest trace of Beliard in the room. Nobody. Gloire even looked for him under the bed. Still, he couldn't have been very far: when she got out of the shower, the bathroom was nothing more than a block of opaque steam. And Beliard's finger being of small format, it was in fine characters that he had traced on the foggy mirror the words SYDNEY–BOMBAY VIA HONG KONG, CATHAY PACIFIC AIRWAYS FLIGHT 112, 10:30. Then, having copied this information onto the back of an envelope, when she went back to change in the bathroom all the moisture was evaporated: the mirror was newly virgin.

But an hour later, at Kingsford Smith Airport, her seat was indeed reserved in club class, smoking section, window—Beliard really could be handy. At ten o'clock, Gloire walked on to the airplane for Bombay dressed in a beige linen suit of vaguely colonial inspiration and shod in summer sandals with rope wedgies. Hardly made up, as had been the case since leaving Brittany, her face was barely visible beneath large black sunglasses and a very concealing bob wig from which, as in the good old days, a few short blonde wisps jutted here and there.

CHAPTER 14

AND THAT SAME DAY, at the other end of the world: "It appears," Salvador continued, "that tall blondes possess an acute awareness of their singularity. This sense of being special, of constituting the product of a mutation, a genetic phenomenon, even a natural castastrophe, can foster a certain tendency toward self-dramatization. Yeah," he said, "anyway. Maybe. What do you think?"

Yawning again, tugging on her skirt with the other hand, Donatienne suggested putting this point off until later, turning instead to some reliable elements in the population under study. For example a little sidebar on Jean Harlow or, I don't know, Doris Day? "All right," said Salvador, "go find me some photos."

Donatienne crossed the room toward the door, gently swaying her hips before the ringed eye of her employer. All around, a sonorous environment in the acute register—car horns from the street, cheeps from the trees, and in the adjoining studios magnetic tapes fast forwarding: the only low note at that moment was Salvador's mood.

As Donatienne turned the knob and pulled the door

open, she nearly ran into Personnettaz who was standing in the hallway behind that same door and who, symmetrically, was pushing it at that very moment. One leaving the room as the other was about to enter, they first took a step back, then, classic misunderstanding, both of them rushed simultaneously into the space freed by the person opposite, jostling each other slightly in the axis of the doorway. Brief, furtive contact, immediately retracted: the man, having inadvertently brushed the young woman's arm, jerked back his own and recoiled. From his desk, Salvador saw the horrified face of Personnettaz, aghast at having touched a high-tension cable, amazed at having survived. Salvador saw Personnettaz's body shaken by strong emotions, as if by one of those twin-release, twin-speed ocean waves that drown you with no questions asked. All this had lasted not three seconds, after which Personnettaz stepped backward, his face suddenly white with fatigue. Donatienne flashed him a candid smile before heading off toward the photo archives.

Personnettaz, looking exhausted, ill at ease, quickly turned away to address Salvador, or rather Salvador's right shoulder, as if he were appraising a stain, three motes of dust, a fallen hair from one of Beliard's cousins.

"Right," he said finally. "We have the information. We know where she is now. We think we know."

"So?" went Salvador. "What are you waiting for?"

"Well, it's far away," said Personnettaz. "It's pretty far away."

"So what?" went Salvador. "What's the problem?"

"Well, it's expensive," said Personnettaz. "The trip, I mean. It's really pretty expensive."

"Of course," sighed Salvador, pulling a checkbook from his drawer. "Business class, I assume?"

"No," said Personnettaz. "Economy will do fine, for two."

While Salvador signs the check and detaches it from its stub, Personnettaz contracts his jaws as Donatienne returns from the archives. She has a sheaf of photographs under her arm as well as a Dunhill, its filter smeared with thick carmine, in the corner of her lips. As she stands leaning next to the open door, waiting for them to finish, Personnettaz pockets the check and rises stiffly. Scrupulously keeping Donatienne just outside his visual field, reaching the exit while describing a discreet arc at a constant distance from her person, he leaves under her still-smiling gaze. But he no longer walks with his natural gait when he knows he is being pursued by a gaze: he stands too awkwardly straight, exaggeratedly contracts his buttocks, his legs parody themselves and his thorax pitches more than necessary; in short, his body follows its own will, and the more he tries to control it the less it obeys. Heading for the elevator, Personnettaz walks like this the entire length of the interminable corridor, sure that Donatienne is still looking at him long after she has shut the door.

As if he were being watched even at a distance, he continued to walk like that on Rue des Martyrs a half hour later, having parked his car on the boulevard. Arriving in front of Boccara's building, he looked up the entrance code in his address book and pressed it in on the keypad next to the street door, several times but in vain: the door remained of stone. Already troubled by Donatienne, Personnettaz felt a nascent exasperation rising in him, made all the sharper by the fact that the nearest phone booth was a good five hundred yards away.

"Personnettaz," he announced. "They gave me a code. What is the code?"

"Er, I don't know, what code have you got?" answered Boccara's intimidated voice.

"Wait a moment," went Personnettaz, leafing one-handedly and with some difficulty through his address book. "They gave me 89-dash-51."

"Ah," went Boccara, "that shows Jouve hasn't been here in a while. Yeah," he recalled, "that 89-dash-51 was a good code, I liked that one. It sounded like a basketball score, and besides it was easy to remember, you know? The French Revolution and Pastis 51, what more could you ask?"

"Fine," said Personnettaz, "so what's the new one?"

"And on top of that, two prime numbers," Boccara continued.

"No," said Personnettaz. "89 is, but not 51. 51 is the product of two primes."

"You're right," said Boccara. "Anyhow, they changed it on us."

"Fine," repeated Personnettaz, "so what's the new one, then?"

"Oh, it's completely ridiculous," said Boccara. "8c603, you see how handy *that* is."

And indeed, once 8c603 was punched in, the low click of the electronic doorman sounded without further ado. Elevator. Mirror at the back of the elevator. Avoid looking at it.

"So," went Boccara, "how's it going? Have you recovered from the other night? I really can't go to bed late like that, I'm bushed. I should also warn you I'm a bit depressed today. Anyway, good thing we found the thing. Some coffee? I've made fresh."

"No," said Personnettaz. "Or actually, sure, why not. Show me the thing."

"Here," said Boccara. "One lump or two?"

The thing consisted of life-size photos of the documents that the two men had found, photographed, then put back in their place in Lagrange's safe: names of foreign cities followed by numerals—dates, addresses, telephone numbers, fax numbers. "Good," said Personnettaz. "We leave tomorrow."

And the next day, Boccara was still saying he was depressed when they boarded the same Boeing for Sydney that Gloire had taken. But we know that she has left Sydney, we already know the deal, so let's get this over with quickly and move on. At the hotel in Darling Harbour they found no one, the weather was miserable, they didn't have time to see anything, they turned back immediately.

In the airplane, Boccara dozed off intermittently. With fifteen hours of flight in one direction, then the other, exhaustion and 180-degree double jet lag, sleep and digestion problems, it didn't help being shaken by nausea when the Boeing hit turbulence. At first demoralized, six hundred miles outside Paris he tried to lift his spirits by resuming the conversation begun several days earlier in the car, on the way back from Brittany. He turned toward Personnettaz, who seemed to be absorbed in the worldwide weather report on the closed-circuit TV.

"It wasn't even true, what I said the other day," Boccara confessed. "The truth is, my sex life stinks. If you knew how sick I am of balling widows in high-rises."

"Well," ventured Personnettaz, "at least there's that."

"You can't imagine what it's like," Boccara continued. "Waking up. The mornings. Going home without even a shower in the highway traffic, in shitty weather, to a freezing apartment. Turning up the heat and keeping your coat on while the coffee perks. You can't imagine how little self-regard that takes."

"So stop seeing them," Personnettaz recommended. "Leave them."

"I never leave anybody," said Boccara. "It's too tiring. All things considered, I'd rather they left me. Keeps me from having to decide. In any case," he developed, "it's never as simple as that. You never really know who's leaving who. You think one of the two is taking the initiative. But the one who's really leaving isn't always the one who seems to be."

That said, Boccara stuck the headphones back into his ears, seeking out a little music among the available programs while toying with the knob embedded in his armrest. Coming upon Shostakovich again, he modified the tilt of his seat the more comfortably to watch the stewardesses at their workstations.

At Roissy, Personnettaz headed for the first booth he saw, but Salvador was still in no mood to answer when the phone rang. On his desk, his main project was again open to the chapter concerning artificial blondes—bleached, peroxide, and so on. "Right," he said quickly, "yes, so it's another bust?" Then, without paying much attention to the other's explanations: "Just a moment."

And leaning toward the pages spread before him, he briefly noted in the margin of one of them that nitrogen peroxide is also used in the manufacture of certain explosives, the propulsion of certain rockets: that could prove useful. Good. Be sure to develop this point.

CHAPTER 15

THAT EVENING AT ELEVEN P.M. IN BOMBAY, in the bar of the Taj Intercontinental, you notice that there are, as in the nightclub in Sydney, very few natives. Almost exclusively foreigners, strangers to the city as they are to each other: strangers squared.

You spot two women who have just entered the bar laughing very freely, laughing as no one ever laughs in a public place; two very gay young women holding a bouquet of large white flowers, which they pass back and forth every five minutes. At first glance you find them beautiful as the light of day, then upon reflection as two different days, two holidays in the heart of opposite seasons.

They had met that same morning on the Sydney-Bombay flight. Seated next to each other by chance, they had traded magazines, cigarettes, and beauty tips, drunk a fair amount, and spoken as only two strangers on a long-distance flight can, thirty-five thousand feet above the rising land masses. Rachel, like Gloire, was traveling alone; like Gloire, she said little about the goals and motives of her enterprise. In the days to come, they would not leave each other's side.

They had arrived in Bombay in late morning with no particular destination in mind, immediately crossed the city in a taxi, then got off at random to pace the streets. They walked through a mass of compact, predominantly sweet odors. Dense like a cumulonimbus with variable geometry, these odors emanated from all sorts of spices, incense, essential oils, and fruits, from flowers and fritters, from smoke, burnt horn, mothballs, and tar, from dust and rot, exhaust and excrement. Then, near Marine Drive, when the young women happened upon some crematoria, the smell of bodies in combustion momentarily blotted out all the others—nuanced, depending on the social class of those bodies, by the scent of the logs between which they went up in smoke: sandalwood or banana for the rich, mango for the hoi polloi. And so they had spent the entire day until dusk.

This evening, alone with your glass at the bar of the Taj, you witness how these two very gay women who have just entered immediately meet—surprise—two men similarly disposed. The gayer of the two immediately chooses the more amusing swain, leaving the other pair to make do as best it can. You watch the scene from afar. It seems to you that this newly constituted foursome does not always express its views in the same language, each member speaking his or her own with copious gestures. You wait a while longer, hesitate, then decide against another drink, and you leave at precisely the moment when, in the mind of the foursome, the idea takes hold that linguistic barriers hardly matter since love is universal. Still, if you were to climb the stairs toward room 212 the following morning at around eleven o'clock and crack open the door, you would find not, as expected, one of those couples, nor the second, but Rachel and Gloire sleeping pressed against each other.

After several days, bored with doing the town, they some-times ended up spending entire days in their room, since they had all the time in the world—always lying close, sleeping (or not) beside the open window on whose ledge perched enormous crows with insolent stares. Rachel had a minuscule tattooed star somewhere, and the crows emit-ted raucous hawkings of the throat like a man about to expectorate. And from morning until night, through that window, rose the voice of some believer droning a sacred air whose harmonies largely resembled those of "Working Class Hero."

Often they did not go out until day's end, after the worst heat had subsided, to take the air near the Elephanta ferry wharf or to buy liquor in some dark stall with a meshed-in window at the back of an alley on the far side of an abandoned building. But near the wharf they also got to know the young men who hung around all day not far from the hotel, between the Taj and the Yacht Club, among the paid ear cleaners. Small fellows who were polite and properly dressed, shadowed by future mustaches and long-term plans; debutant businessmen who gravely spread the fan of their wares—substances to inhale, substances to inject, boys and girls to fuck, bills to change. Without resorting to their services, Rachel hit it off with a receiv-er named Biplab, apparently fell in love with him, and dis-appeared a few days later—exiting Gloire's life as suddenly as she had entered.

After that, alone in Bombay, it was different; the city seemed noisier. Gloire spent two full days without leaving the hotel, wasting her time with the boutique keepers on the ground floor. When she tried going out once on the third day, several beggars pursued her more aggressively than usual, emitting the same throaty calls as the crows; legless cripples launched in her wake cut her off from behind. Gloire returned to her room passably demoralized. She was starting to miss Beliard. He had not shown his face the entire time she was with Rachel—understandably. Still, now that she was alone again, the least he could do was reappear. But no. She began to wonder whether the homunculus, finding a better opportunity, hadn't stayed behind in Sydney.

Whatever the case, the best thing to do was go away again. Rachel had spoken to her of a town in the south where life seemed mellow, and of a quiet, genteel, English-style residence. Gloire had jotted down the address. She had the concierge reserve her a seat, in air-conditioned class, on the next train heading south, and left the following morning.

A quiet little town, in these latitudes, means at least a million feverish inhabitants, but the Cosmopolitan Club was a venerable institution located on the outskirts of the center, in the legations neighborhood. Its main entrance adjoined the Burmese consulate and, in back, a rear gate looking out on the corner of Cenotaph Road and Archbishop Vincent Street led to a residential stretch of great white villas bordered by gardens, enclosed by walls. There Gloire could feel sheltered.

A wide, low building, the Cosmopolitan Club was composed of a huge foyer and several salons, a restaurant, a smoking parlor, bridge-, pool-, and ballrooms, a bar, another bar, a third bar. Its roof terrace was capped by a dodecagonal pinnacle, topped by an infundibuliform urn. Decorated with official photos of the Queen and other, more recent ones of the Prince of Wales, the foyer extended into a porch and then beneath a pale cement canopy, under which heavy Ambassador limousines and big-engined Hindustanis discharged the club's empty-stomached members by the hour, before repocketing them soused to the gills a quart or two later. To the left was a swimming pool filled with fresh water, to the right a library filled with stale volumes. Then an isolated building, with two floors of rooms and suites served by a rosewood elevator: that was where Gloire would stay, not far from the side entrance with its unimpeded view of Cenotaph Road. All of it in a silken silence, even if from the bustling neighborhoods farther on came a monotonous rumble, hardly noticeable but uninterrupted, acrid like a guilty conscience and giving the silence its contour.

The establishment was like a cross between a luxury hotel, a family pension, and a sanatorium. Unchanged since British times, the bars were mahogany, the wall lamps copper, the silverware silver, the tennis courts red clay, and the servants white. Visible from the restaurant dining room, beyond a porch as long and wide as the upper deck of an ocean liner, fifteen gentle stairs led down to a park planted with peepuls and margosas, populated with mongeese and parrots, bordered by a river prone to flooding. The sun was shining. Perfect.

Immediately upon Gloire's arrival, the superintendent showed her to her room. Exaggeratedly large, it was equipped with a black and white Texla television, a sky-blue refrigerator, and a huge air conditioner between the two windows, with three fans on the ceiling. Above each nightstand, four little glass mounts displayed little birds (*Chloropsis cochinchinensis*), while a large glass mount above the bed depicted four large birds (*Porphyrio porphyrio*). Better and better.

The superintendent, a thin young man with a fine, cold mustache and fine, icy smile, disappeared the minute she signed the register. In the following days he would prove to be very discreet, not so much absent as fleeting. On the other hand, the somewhat aged bellboys proved exceedingly attentive. The wife of the nicest bellboy, the one in charge of the morning ministrations, was temporarily in the hospital, so Gloire slipped him two thousand rupees. Then, once she had hung her clothes in closets a hundred times too big, walked around the park, crisscrossed the empty salons, and gotten her bearings, her days began to take shape.

Each one the same. At seven A.M., the heat awoke her. A little before eight, the hospitalized woman's husband set the tray with morning tea on a low table and drew back the curtains. Sliding together along the curtain rods, the metal rings rang *zing zing,* to the left, to the right, like a knife being sharpened. Gloire then ate her breakfast on the balcony, alone, occasionally tossing to the ground fragments of toast that were coveted equally by the numerous giant crows and ground squirrels that charged onto them all in a heap. Nine times out of ten the squirrels beat a retreat before the arrogance of the crows, more powerful and better organized, beneath circles that eagles described in the sky. After that, Gloire rested a moment in her room, seeing nothing before her but two lizards, short, pink, and immobile on the wall. Only once did she try to catch one.

A number of rickshaws were permanently stationed by the gate, ready to transport the club's pensioners. Gloire took the first one she saw—a yellow scooter with hastily suspended roof, three wheels, two seats in back, and a nonworking meter—toward the center of town. She lingered a moment at the fabric merchants', in the temples, or at the massage parlors, daily entrusting her hands to specialists, surface and depth, chiromancer and manicurist by turns.

Not without curiosity, the locals watched her, unaccustomed to tall blondes; few of them grow in those climates. Meanwhile, far away, Salvador jotted down vague ideas on the subject—tall blondes in Austin Minis, tall blondes and scorched-earth policy—while keeping in the corner of his eye, just in case, the reproduction of a work by Jim Dine entitled *The Blonde Girls* (oil, charcoal, rope, 1960). At the same time, Personnettaz labored, in vain for the moment, to pick up the trail of Gloire who was spending her afternoons on a poolside lounge chair, if she wasn't taking a stroll around the park, stopping at times by the generator near the pond, in which a hundred calm toads, at all hours, silently snapped up any insect below a certain caliber.

In the evenings, Gloire dined alone in the restaurant, a book open on her table and eating with one eye. Then she went to bed early in front of the television, following a Tamil film that wasn't too hard to understand or, turning off the sound, picking up one of the books borrowed from the library, most often encyclopedic works, travel narratives, natural history manuals, studies of customs, or more specialized treatises published by Thacker, Spink & Co. (Calcutta), such as *Animals of No Importance* or *Dogs for Warm Climates.* All of this Gloire read methodically, neither skipping nor retaining a single line. Then, in theory, she went to sleep—although it wasn't always easy, and soon less and less easy to get there. As for Beliard, he still hadn't appeared since Sydney. A problem with his passport, perhaps?

CHAPTER 16

THE FOLLOWING WEEK HER INSOMNIA INTENSIFIED. It gnawed Gloire's sleep from both ends, morning and evening in equal measure, deducting a few supplementary minutes every night. Every day, Gloire woke up more tired than before.

At the club bar, she ended up meeting a few Europeans, resident or transient, in particular British subjects representing their firms: an insurance underwriter for the crown jewels, a perfume salesman, an engineer specializing in brakes—a largely neglected device, unknown in these latitudes where they prefer the horn, and thus a huge potential market.

But she spent little time in the bar. In the evenings, to stave off the hour when she would attempt sleep, Gloire stayed awhile by the pond near the gate. After having snapped up every possible animalcule during the day, the toads were now digesting, singing placidly in chorus. To execute their little concert, they split up into three sections, some reproducing the squawkings of fowl, others a police siren, still others a Morse transmitter: a frenetic, simultaneous chorus, without a moment's respite, Morse and siren at an octave's remove, the deep breath of the generator serving at once as continuous bass and pitch pipe. Above the batrachian chorales, from the branches of a rain tree, a winged soloist sometimes projected a brief, melodic utterance in counterpoint, a few riffs in third. Gloire listened for a quarter of an hour, then headed inside to go to bed.

Sometimes she was invited, and sometimes she accepted offers to join the British subjects, who organized parties on Tuesday evenings, dancing the cakewalk on the terrace in Adidas and Bermuda shorts, sweating amid the bottle-laden tables. On one such evening, and one evening only, Gloire let herself go so far as to empty five or six glasses at a shot.

After which she returned stone drunk to the club, where she spent a ridiculous amount of time looking for her room key, then for the lock, and then, once inside, for the night-light switch. She emitted a brief cry after thinking she'd made out, in the semidarkness, a small oblong shape across her bed. Then she got a grip, tried to reason with herself: poor old girl, you're still completely sloshed. But no: at the sound of the slammed door the little shape suddenly bolted upright, stiff as a poker and with arms crossed, looking cross.

"Do you see what time it is?" shouted Beliard. "Is this any time to be getting home?"

"Miserable little shit," said Gloire. "You scared me."

"That's only the beginning," Beliard cried still louder. "If you ask me, things have been getting pretty lax around here. I'm going to have to take things back in hand, you bet I am."

"You're such a shit," Gloire repeated, spotting a chair in the shadows and collapsing into it, a hand over her eyes.

"Watch what you say," cautioned Beliard in a sharp though less assured voice.

"Couldn't you let me know you were coming?" she said after a while, standing with difficulty to go pour herself a last drink.

"I'm not kidding," Beliard tried to threaten, pointing a finger at her glass, then wagging that finger. "You'll get what's coming to you if you don't watch it."

"This is insane," said Gloire. "I haven't seen you in ages. Never there when I need you. I could have dropped dead ten times over."

"I come by when I can," claimed the homunculus, letting his defenses down. "Do you think this is all I have to do? Did you see how I look? With the jet lag, the trip, and all? If you think I'm doing it for fun," he said, pulling a small mirror from his pocket. "I mean it—do you see what I look like?"

And in fact, he was pale and disheveled, suit rumpled, tie and laces undone. And he hadn't shaved. "I can't take it anymore," he groaned, falling back onto the bed. Gloire took a sip from her glass and watched him lying there disarticulated, a cheap doll.

"So what were you up to?" she said. "Where were you? Did you stay behind in Sydney?"

"Let me sleep," yawned Beliard. "I think I need to sleep."

"Lucky you," she said. "I can't even close my eyes anymore. You don't want to know the kind of nights I've spent."

"I'll take care of that," muttered Beliard. "We'll see about that tomorrow."

"Yeah, sure," said Gloire.

But the next morning Beliard was still asleep when she went out, as she did every day, to take a spin around town. Among the rickshaws posted at the club entrance, she had finally settled on a vehicle that looked better maintained than the others, the apparent object of its pilot's devotion. Decorated with lit cones of camphor, it sported a little altar of flowers and statuettes hung over the vehicle's handlebars, above which, on the windshield, were several decals of deities. Painted on the rear of the machine near the reflectors, two mascaraed eyes squinted at a government slogan preaching birth control and, under a roof all patched with duct tape, on either side of the rear seat, were two identical portraits depicting an actor, or a politician, or more likely one and the same.

As for the driver of this rickshaw, he was a friendly, rotund young man named Sanjeev, with linen shirt and pants, and a faded pink cotton handkerchief around his neck. After their first trip, he had offered to put himself exclusively at Gloire's service. His hair was cropped close, except for a long lock on the back of his skull, a handle for pulling him from Hell in case he fell in. He was friendly and very even tempered; he drove well, his meter worked, and his incense was of good quality. Gloire had answered why not. The only problem with him: his chronic cold made him sneeze constantly and blow his nose at every red light into his pink handkerchief, which also served as headband, scarf, belt, compress, rag, bath towel, table napkin, and shopping bag.

When she returned to her room after lunch, Gloire was once more extremely pale, and Beliard showed some alarm. "Get a little rest," he suggested before going back to sleep himself, "try to take a nap." She tried, but sleep no longer existed. It was the same once night had fallen, and again all the following nights, until one fine morning found her utterly exhausted, hardly able to move.

Obviously incapable of treating Gloire's insomnia, Beliard mainly took care of catching up on his own delayed slumber. She spent her days next to him as he slept, lying in her room with the curtains drawn. Staring at the ceiling, no longer thinking of anything, counting the fan's revolutions unto infinity.

For those three days she ventured out of her room only at mealtimes, leaving her breakfasts unfinished, hidden behind dark glasses. As soon as she got up, the crows would swoop down onto the leftovers and divvy up toast, sugar, butter, and artificial marmalade before flying off again to savor their delicacies in peace, motionless on the blade of a fan.

And then there was one evening, at the club restaurant, when Gloire jumped on discovering a very agitated spider in a spoon resting on its convex bowl next to her plate. The imprisoned insect turned around and around, struggled in the bottom of the utensil. An instant of revulsion seized her before she saw wriggling in that concavity only the reflection of another fan above her.

Fans, it appeared, were beginning to occupy too much space in her life. But only at the end of a week, worn out by her sleepless nights, when she began seeing fat frozen mosquitoes in the filaments of electric lightbulbs, did she begin to worry. Beliard, declaring himself unequal to the task, threw up his hands. Gloire confided her troubles to the bellboys.

The bellboys, who had a soft spot for her—a friendly, reserved young woman, not too tight with her rupees, rarely stayed out too late at the bar—the bellboys were very sorry to hear it. After they'd consulted with each other, the hospitalized woman's husband took the plunge and slipped a word to the superintendent. A diagonal smile lightly capsized the mustache of the superintendent, who finally jotted on the back of his card the address of a local practitioner who had a clinic at 33 Karaneeswarar Sannadhi Street, at the corner of a particularly commercial artery.

Beliard, meanwhile, who had not left the room, had been sleeping practically nonstop since his return. Gloire shook him before leaving:

"I'm going out," she told him. "I think I might have found someone for my insomnia."

"We'll see about that," grunted the homunculus, turning over.

Then she went out into the heaviest afternoon heat. Near the gate, in the shade, the rickshaw drivers were asleep at their handlebars. "No problem," said Sanjeev after deciphering the address, before turning the ignition.

They arrived. Squeezed one against the other was an abundance of shops: sellers of pumps, springs, hoses, hardware, plaster, and rope; electricians, plumbers, barbers—the same shops, in short, as anywhere else in the world, except that, not being larger than sixty square feet, all these establishments looked alike under their roofs of braided palm leaves, planks, and straw, and on their packed-earth floors.

Once Sanjeev had dropped her off, Gloire had difficulty finding the doctor's address: the neighborhood buildings, first of all, were not particularly well numbered, and then the contents of the shops didn't always match their signs. So that when she finally located the plaque mentioning Dr. Gopal's clinic, it was attached to the front of a music store in which two men with painted foreheads were arguing bitterly without any trace around them of scores, instruments, or recordings.

She hesitated: on the sidewalk to the left, a stall contained two facing machines, one for typing, one for sewing; while to the right, another offered Xerox-telex-fax services. Above, in back, balancing on scaffoldings made of rope and bamboo, two painters were sketching the design of an advertising panel whose object was still not very clear: liquor or cigarettes, a television or perhaps a washing machine. Sanjeev went to ask the manager of the Xerox-telex-fax, who pointed out the clinic's location: at the back of a courtyard past an L-shaped passage, across from a temple devoted to the goddess of smallpox.

The clinic's reception area, though filled with fans and rugs at death's door, nonetheless boasted state-of-the-art communications equipment. A young woman with a pearl embedded in the wing of her nose and a ring on the third toe of each foot was monitoring the clientele on a screen. As soon as he was informed of Gloire's presence, Gopal appeared, wearing a gigantic gem on his right index finger.

Moreover, despite the manners of an archbishop, the doctor was a bit slovenly-looking: checkered blouse floating over a green-striped loincloth casually knotted in front, People's Republic of China thongs on his feet. Profusely oiled salt-and-pepper hair curling in ringlets over the nape of his neck, large glasses with marbled frames and lenses so strong that one could see no more of his eyes than two pupils and two irises multiplied by ten.

Once Gloire had explained her problem, she and Gopal exchanged routine questions and answers in English— overall health, childhood illnesses, family history, nature of the symptoms. Gopal showed sympathy for this problem, which could, he said, be remedied with the appropriate ayurvedic mixture. Rifling through a drawer in his desk, he pulled out a box of brown pills, counted out a few, and slid them into a brown paper bag, one at bedtime for ten days and that should do it, a thousand rupees.

As soon as Gloire left the clinic, Gopal dialed the superintendent's personal line. Outside, Sanjeev was waiting for the young woman. "Good doctor?" he asked.

"He doesn't seem too bad," said Gloire. "You should see him about that cold."

"Expensive," said Sanjeev. "Much too expensive for me."

"Here," said the young woman, rummaging through her bag.

"Thank you," said Sanjeev. "That's a lot."

"Not for me," said Gloire.

So no sooner had he brought her back to the Cosmopolitan Club than Sanjeev returned to the clinic at top speed. Gloire, meanwhile, entered her room. Still lying in the same place, Beliard was no longer sleeping; he seemed to have rested, shaved, changed, refreshed himself. He asked about Gloire's doings.

"I wouldn't recommend you keep seeing that guy, if you want my opinion," he advised a little later, pouring the brown pills into his diminutive hand. "If I were you, I wouldn't trust that guy."

That guy, meanwhile, was examining Sanjeev lengthily and minutely: apart from his chronic head cold, apparently of allergic origin, the young man seemed to enjoy excellent health.

"I see what the problem is," he said. "I'm going to prescribe a little product that will surely make you happy."

At the back of another drawer in his desk, Gopal went in search of a vial filled with powder that was also brown, of which he poured a few grains into a sheet of paper folded in eight to form a flat envelope. "Here you go," he prescribed. "Two or three times a day by nasal inhalation and that should do it, ten rupees."

Sanjeev returned to the club and settled into the backseat of his vehicle to inhale a little of the powder, per the doctor's orders. In fact, he immediately felt much better, slumping on his seat and letting his gaze float toward the window behind which Gloire and Beliard were discussing the future. And began, when you got down to it, to find that time passed awfully slowly.

CHAPTER 17

TO BOCCARA'S BIG BLUE EYES, AS WELL, time passed slowly. Nothing to do in life these days except walk up and down Rue des Martyrs, awaiting instructions from Personnettaz.

At the moment, he was walking down. Under his soles creaked and cracked fragments of broken, sometimes smoked safety glass, scattered into little beaches on the sidewalks and in the gutters, flanking vehicles freshly relieved of their radios. He stopped in front of a tattoo parlor whose window displayed a whole range of samples. Alongside lesser designs for the timorous—little flowers, small animals—larger subjects reserved for the true aficionado depicted entire scenes, queens of the night, heroes of the jungle, or body-built leopards. Tempted at first, Boccara finally resisted. In any case, his watch informed him that it was time, from the first booth he saw, to place his daily call to Personnettaz.

The latter seemed to have picked up Gloire's traces without the young man's help: they were leaving tomorrow. "It's pretty far again this time," he said. "Not as far as last time, but pretty far all the same."

"Hold on a minute," said Boccara. "Where exactly are we going?" (His eyes widened.) "What?" (He inhaled sharply.) "Hey, hang on there, nothing doing. The place is crawling with filthy diseases. When will I have time to get my shots?"

"Don't worry," said Personnettaz, "I've looked into that. It's no longer necessary."

"And what about swamp fever?" Boccara pointed out. "That's a whole preventative treatment right there, swamp fever. With all those mosquitoes, and the humidity besides, and the rain. It rains there all the time. I know."

"I've looked into that," repeated the other wearily. "Monsoon season is over. If anything, it should be rather hot."

"Oh, well then," Boccara mused, "so light cotton clothes. Even so, I'm going to try and borrow a mosquito net. And anyway, you never know with the rain, I'll bring my slicker."

"That's right," said Personnettaz, "bring your slicker."

Given the number of airplanes we've already taken, and the others we might still have to take, no sense describing the one they boarded the next day. In any case, it had nothing special about it. Air India, your basic 747, with no distinguishing features other than the mealtime choice of vegetarian or not, the coral-colored saris of the stewardesses, the leafy carpet with matching elevator music.

No, nothing special, except that when they landed in Delhi, Personnettaz spotted an unusual phenomenon off in the distance. As he was waiting behind Boccara in the customs line, he noticed that a small crowd was amassing immediately past the booth: a group smiling from ear to ear, though official in appearance, comprised of civilian aviation uniforms and administrative suits, surrounded by flowers and crowned by an incomprehensible streamer, with a few words in Hindi yellowing together on a wire. Personnettaz gritted his teeth when the lively stares and wide smiles at first seemed to be aimed his way. Then as they moved closer it became evident that it wasn't *him* they had trained their sights on, but Boccara. Airsick, not feeling very well, one hand on his abdomen and the other over his lips, the aforementioned Boccara shuffled forward without noticing a thing.

As soon as the young man passed through customs, there was a simultaneous explosion of flashbulbs and applause, accompanied by a brief fanfare. A short, enthusiastic individual with a mustache and dark suit rushed up and warmly pumped Boccara's hand, while with his other hand he groped for the glasses in his pocket and with a third hand reached into another pocket for a scrap of paper that he unfolded and began to read. Boccara, whose mastery of English left something to be desired, spun around in wild-eyed panic.

"What's going on?"

Personnettaz nervously rolled his passport like a last, empty pack of cigarettes.

"He says you're the millionth passenger to take this flight," he translated. "He says they've planned a celebration."

"So?"

"So I suspect we won't be seeing each other for a while."

And, in fact, after the congratulations the short man enumerated all the various advantages, gifts, and cruises of which Boccara had just become the lucky beneficiary. When they slipped the first garland of flowers around his assistant's neck, Personnettaz rolled his eyes heavenward. Alone in his aisle seat in the airplane heading back, he was in no mood to describe the flight either.

Paris. Beastly cold and raining cats and dogs. Everyone bundled up in a swinish mood. Even Donatienne, unusually covered, looking not very inviting, has kept her coat on in the office.

"I'm drawing a bit of a blank with these tall blondes," Salvador observes.

"We've been drawing a blank with everything," she says, "since the beginning."

"No angle, I've lost my angle," says Salvador. "Do measurements make for an angle? What do you think of Jayne Mansfield? Or how about an extraterrestrial angle? Something like this: You always thought they'd be little green men. Wrong! They're tall blonde girls."

Donatienne prefers to reserve comment, and it is in silence that two knocks sound on the door, which opens immediately afterward to reveal Personnettaz. The man's features are drawn, his eyes too shiny, his mouth bitter. The man seems tired. He has psychologically prepared himself not to cast a single glance at Donatienne, but he can't help sneaking a few sidelong peeks. His peripheral vision registers a coat. The man finds this oddly reassuring. "Well, Personnettaz," says Salvador. "I thought you were far away."

"I've lost Boccara," says Personnettaz.

Salvador stares at him without comprehending, reestablishing the silence that is immediately pierced in a very shrill register by Donatienne's laughter. Personnettaz, while explaining the facts, forces himself not to train on her the eyes of the assassin that he isn't, having failed the test for that profession.

"Can't you keep looking on your own?" Salvador asks.

"It's not the way I operate," says Personnettaz. "I only work with an assistant. I'd be happy to continue, but you'll have to find me another assistant."

"That's not really in my line," says Salvador. "I don't see anyone around here who could..." To Donatienne: "*You* don't have any ideas, do you?"

"Sure I do," says Donatienne.

"You see?" says Salvador. "That's what's so great about her, she always comes up with good ideas. Who do you have in mind?"

"Me," says Donatienne.

"My gosh what a great idea," says Salvador.

"Wait a minute," says Personnettaz, "please. I'd rather not."

"I'll see about the schedules," Donatienne is already organizing, "Odile will see about tickets and Gerard about the visa, it's always faster with Gerard."

"Please," repeats Personnettaz. "Listen to me for two seconds."

But no one is listening to him anymore. His life is about to change, he can see it, he can feel it, he is going to regret it. Boccara annoyed him no end, but Boccara will be missed. Boccara for whom it's surely the good life, flying first-class from palace to palace, thick as thieves with the crew, clinking glasses by the dozen with the pilots, the stereo cranked up full, pulling the stewardesses into the lavatory and doing lines with the steward during the night flights, in the galley while everyone is asleep.

Speaking of which, on Karaneeswarar Sannadhi Street, Sanjeev has just returned to Dr. Gopal's office: "So, feeling better?" the latter asks. "Are you happy with your treatment?"

"Much better," answers Sanjeev. "Very happy, doctor."

And indeed, he seems genuinely happy to be feeling better. His eyes are pink with pleasure, his pupils contracted with joy. His stare is fixedly satisfied. "Really much better," he insists. "I'd like to get some more of that medicine."

"That should not be difficult," says the doctor. "I do believe it's the right thing for you. We're moving along nicely toward a cure, so we're going to modify the dosage accordingly. Increase the amount a little bit. This time I'm going to give you ten grams of the medicine."

"Ten grams isn't much," Sanjeev seems to remember.

"See for yourself," the doctor tells him, thrusting the tips of his fingers into his drawer.

He pulls out a paper envelope folded the same as the other day, but five or six times fatter. Ten grams is much more than Sanjeev thought. Sanjeev is delighted.

"And in addition, you're going to discontinue the inhalations," the doctor prescribes. "I'll show you how to inject it, it's very simple."

"If you say so, doctor," says Sanjeev. "How can I ever thank you?"

"It's nothing," says the doctor, "don't thank me. As you see, it's still ten rupees; I ask nothing in return. Well, actually, perhaps just a little of your blood—you see, it isn't much. You don't mind, I trust?"

"As much as you want," Sanjeev hesitates.

"This must remain strictly between us," Gopal specifies. "It's blood, you see. It's a little like a pact."

"Of course," Sanjeev nods gravely.

"So it's nothing at all, I'll take just a little quart. No objections?"

"No problem," says Sanjeev.

"And then you can come back here as often as you like," says Gopal. "Now, roll up your sleeve for me."

CHAPTER 18

"THAT BOY'S IN PITIFUL SHAPE," Beliard observed a few days later.

Through the open window, with scale-model binoculars, he watched Sanjeev sprawled over the handlebars of his vehicle in full sunlight, among the green plants by the gate of the Cosmopolitan Club. "Don't you think you should go see what's wrong with him?"

Thanks to Gopal's care, Gloire had found sleep again and had stopped being quite so interested in ceiling fans. It was the middle of siesta time: "Don't feel like it," she mumbled without opening an eye. "Fuck off."

"Go on, I'm telling you," Beliard insisted. "I really think there's something wrong with him."

She yawned as she skirted the library toward the parking area reserved for rickshaws. Following the passage of cargo planes, the sky above her head was crossed out by jet exhaust, stitched with white gashes that quickly scarred. Boughs of albizzias shuddered gently in their wake and the toads, at peace in the pond, continued to absorb their animalcules. Gloire crossed through the gate, paused for a moment: from that angle, Sanjeev really did-n't look too chipper.

It's true that the young man's services had fallen off a bit recently. Things weren't going well. Contained for two or three days, his cold had not only returned full-blown but was worsening exponentially. He now hunched over when he coughed. Even his wonderful composure was vis-ibly sprouting cracks. Less assiduous, less precise, Sanjeev proved to be more irritable, bitter about his earnings, even secretive. Nonetheless, he still placed enough trust in Gloire—when she came up to shake him gently, ask him if everything was all right, and then, while they were at it, question him delicately about his recent changes of habit—to designate Gopal's medicine as the probable cause, together with the sustained rhythm of his blood donations. Having been quickly initiated into the admin-istration of intravenous injections, his life was no more than a to-and-fro of syringes in both directions. Gloire studied him fixedly, without saying anything at first. "Wait for me here," she then said. "I'll be right back."

"I told you not to trust that guy," Beliard reminded her after she recapped the situation. "You see what he's capa-ble of. Although, when you get down to it, he didn't do such a bad job with you. Hey, what are you up to now?"

"I'm changing," said Gloire, haphazardly pulling three pieces of clothing from a closet. "You were right, but we can't just let it go. The doctor has some explaining to do."

Beliard covered his forehead with his hand: is she crazy or what? "I strongly advise you against it," he said as if it were obvious. "Don't get mixed up in that. What's done is done. Let it be. Don't go. Wait. Come back. Hey, come back!" But twenty minutes later, bathed in sweat, eyes bulging, Sanjeev dropped Gloire on Karaneeswarar Sannadhi Street.

Gopal received her immediately, gaze as voluminous as ever behind his glasses, stucco smile. Without a word she sat down opposite him. "I can see right away that you're feeling better," said the practitioner. "You look much better. I believe the treatment is the right thing for you. We will continue the cure, but today I would like for us to begin with a little relaxation. Relaxation is very good for insomnia."

"I'll give you some bloody relaxation," answered Gloire, "you lousy prick."

"I beg your pardon?" said Gopal.

"You're a complete shit," she continued. "I know what you're doing with the kid."

"The kid?" went Gopal.

"The kid with the rickshaw," Gloire specified.

"Which one?" smiled Gopal.

"You're disgusting," Gloire insisted. "I should turn you in and have you locked up. In fact, I *am* going to turn you in and have you locked up."

"I see," said Gopal, calmly noting this new symptom on a pad, "very well." He was silent for a moment. "I see what the problem is," he finally said. "I understand. But I'm afraid that would not be in your best interests. Let me notify my associate."

"I'm warning you," said Gloire, "don't try anything. They know I'm here."

"Naturally," said the practitioner, "have no fear. My associate will explain everything." Stretching a finger toward the fat telephone, he pressed a button: immediately, at the other end of the room, a curtain pulled aside. Electrified line of mustache, gelatinous smile, and sharp eye, the thin silhouette of the superintendent appeared.

Two hours later, Beliard was lounging on the bed in his underwear when Gloire walked in. Her light makeup was undone; her first movement was to rush over to the mini-bar and pour herself a drink. "What happened to you?" asked the homunculus. "You should see your face."

Trembling, she aimed poorly, letting the liquor spill next to her glass. "You can't imagine," she said, "you'd never guess."

"I think I would," Beliard said calmly. "You ran into the superintendent, am I right?"

Although in principle he has only the information that Gloire gives him on her comings and goings, it indeed seems that Beliard, through other sources or double vision, is aware of all or part of the young woman's life. The young woman is sitting on the bed, no longer paying attention. "Tell me about it anyway," he says. Well, it's like this. They had done their homework, they seemed to know everything. They knew someone was after her. The inquiries seemed to have been led by the superintendent, who had communicated his information on Gloire to Gopal. Suggesting to her that they were hand in glove with the local police, the two men had threatened her with serious troubles if she tried to interfere.

"But," Beliard exclaimed, "you *did* tell them you've paid your debt, didn't you? You have nothing more to blame yourself for, in theory. No one has any reason to be after you."

Of course she had told them. But: "And what would prevent us from, say, becoming interested in your little visit to Australia?" Gopal had pointed out. Gloire did not have full control of her voice when she asked him what he meant. ("Very clever," commented Beliard.) "I don't mean anything in particular," Gopal had smiled. "We're talking, that's all. We're talking about you, and we can make others talk about you, but we won't do that. We might be needing you."

"What?" Gloire had repeated. "What do you mean? For what?" ("Better and better," noted Beliard.)

"We'll see," Gopal had told her. "You'll see—we'll be seeing each other again. There you have it."

Beliard thought for a moment, then shrugged his shoulders. "He's bluffing about Australia," he said. "Nobody could know about that. I know, I was there. Nobody. They can't do anything to you."

He ran the edge of a fingernail between his two yellowest teeth, glanced briefly at his catch.

"Of course, there might still be a way," he continued. "You want to get rid of them? You know we could always do it. The usual method, a little precipice and sayonara."

"No," said Gloire, "we can't. There are too many of them, and I'm afraid they're well organized."

They certainly were. All day long the many servants passed through their lodging under the slightest pretext, to water the plants and clean the room, to bring tea, the morning papers, the afternoon papers with still more tea, the laundry, mosquito coils in the evening. Every bellboy seemed a likely informant for Gopal via the superintendent.

The following days were not very jolly. Gloire now spoke only to Beliard, put no more trust in anybody; she began to suspect the librarian, even the hospitalized woman's husband. As at the height of her insomnia the week before, she went back to staying in her room, keeping the door closed to the staff, heading down to eat only when everyone was taking his afternoon nap.

But alas, not everyone was napping. One afternoon, as she was leaving the restaurant at around three o'clock, she noticed Gopal and the superintendent leaning against the adjacent bar. The two men seemed engrossed in serious conversation. Gloire made herself as scarce as possible, passing like a shadow a good distance away. But if Gopal was blind as a bat, the superintendent wasn't. After a quick glance, he whispered briefly to the practitioner, who brusquely turned toward the young woman. "What a delightful surprise!" he said. "Will you take a little refreshment with us?"

But there was nothing refreshing about his statements. "You're just the person I wanted to see," he claimed. "You can't refuse. I'd like to entrust you with an object that I wish to have delivered to my cousin in Bombay. You know that the mail here," he chuckled, "is a little like in your Italy. I'd rather have it delivered by hand, by private courier. Does that sound like something you'd care to handle? We'll pay for the trip, of course."

"I see what this is about," said Gloire.

"I'm sure you do," said Gopal, "but I believe you'll do it anyway."

"No chance," said Gloire.

"No reason to be suspicious," Gopal impressed upon her. "It doesn't commit you to anything, there's no risk involved; naturally I'll reimburse you. All the more so in that, from what I understand, it would not be a bad idea for you to go away for a few days."

Gloire stood up. "What does that mean?"

"I'm just telling you what I know," answered Gopal, "just giving my opinion."

"Let me think about it," she said.

"But of course," said Gopal, "think about it. Even if it won't change anything, it's the least I can offer."

Back in her room, she consulted Beliard.

"We could have seen it coming," he said. "All right, so what do we do?"

"You tell me," she went. "You're the one with the bright ideas."

"My idea is that we do it," said Beliard. "It'll be a change of scenery. And besides," he asked, "what do we have to lose, at this point?"

"I don't know," she said. "Whatever you say."

"Yes," said Beliard, "might as well go away for a while. And besides, we'll be better off in Bombay. It's bigger, more anonymous; they'll leave us alone. Anyway, I've never been to Bombay. Is it nice?"

She didn't answer right away. Sitting crosswise on the bed, legs folded, she thumbed through a copy of the *Bhagavad Gita,* left with a Bible as fixtures on the bedside table.

"Where were you?" she said.

"What, where?" Beliard conjuncted. "When?"

"When I was in Bombay, where were you? Did you really stay in Sydney?"

"Don't get on my case about that," said Beliard. "You know damn well we never talk about that. I have a right to my own life. Go tell him we'll do it."

Then, once Gloire was back in the bar: "I never doubted it for a moment," said Gopal. "Well, then, you leave tomorrow morning."

"So soon?"

"Believe me," said Gopal, "it's in your best interests."

CHAPTER 19

AS TACTLESS, DUPLICITOUS, AND CORRUPT as Dr. Gopal surely was, for once at least he hadn't been lying. The following afternoon, a rented purple Ambassador limousine, sans air conditioner, rolled gently down Cenotaph Road in the direction of the Cosmopolitan Club.

Cenotaph Road is a calm little artery, residential albeit dusty, almost an alley bordered by tall acacias that surge from intertwined bushes. Every hundred yards, an enormous white villa succeeds another, its flat roof capped with a parabolic antenna, its gateway topped with a sign warning visitors against dogs (although one never sees any dogs), and flanked by a booth containing a dozing watchman in unbuttoned paramilitary khaki uniform, belt, badge, and tilted beret. Surrounded by gardens and shut in by walls, these villas never exceed two floors, embellished with terraces featuring steps, turrets, verandahs, and canopies protected by blinds, tarpaulins, screens, or modern variations on moucharaby.

One does not meet many inhabitants of these residences. Sometimes, in the distance, silhouettes clad in light-colored pajamas quickly cross the street from one gate to another. The domestics, no doubt. Beneath a balcony, behind fences braided with shrubbery, a solo, bald, myopic old man with a mustache lets himself be carried back and forth on a swing of feeble amplitude. But as you look at him he looks at you, and you lower your eyes. The temperature nears ninety-five degrees. Everything is calm, almost nothing to be heard. A great white light wears down the contours and colors of things, to the point of confiscating one of their three dimensions. In short, it's Sunday.

At the moment, the Ambassador was the only vivid object in this pale world. Driving at low speed, it encountered few people as it passed. A cyclist transported a bin much too large for his conveyance, but five minutes later another cyclist transported two bins that were just as large. Three women from the less plentiful neighborhoods bound dead branches of casuarina into faggots. From level ground to blue heaven, butterflies flitted, parakeets fluttered, and squadrons of crows darted. A couple of homosexual ground squirrels, before getting down to it in the gutter, risked pusillanimous pecks with their snouts, left, right, left, etc.

Two circling eagles were reflected in the Ambassador's roof, beneath which three individuals were thinking, each in his own way, about different subjects such as sex, for instance, or money. The Western man seated in back was thinking vaguely, still dressed in his wrinkled straw-colored suit. The woman seated next to him—light-colored cotton ensemble bought two days earlier at a tropical outfitter's in Paris—was thinking more dreamily. Only the native chauffeur, in linen slacks and shirt with a dirty front, was speculating more forwardly about the measurements of that lady and the revenues of that gentleman.

The gentleman uttered two brief words just before Cenotaph Road met a narrow private drive that disappeared, after a bend, beneath a mango tree; they turned onto it. Having good visibility, they saw that in the distance, at the location of a gateway, this drive was closed off by cement speed blocks next to which, parallel to the raised barrier, a bilingual sign informed the public of the interdiction to enter the Cosmopolitan Club, and of the prosecution that would befall all trespassers. Following two more brief words, the car stopped fifty yards before the threshold.

"Right," said Personnettaz, "I think this is it. I'm going in. Wait for me here."

"I beg your pardon," said Donatienne, "but I'm coming with you."

"No no no no," Personnettaz inflected in various tones, "this part of the job has always been my responsibility."

"But I have to be there," Donatienne insisted, "that's what I'm here for. Otherwise, what good am I?"

"Don't insist," Personnettaz settled the matter. "Besides, you don't have the proper training."

"Stupid jerk," Donatienne muttered as soon as he'd slammed the door. "If that's how he's going to be, maybe I'll just get it on with the chauffeur." But in the final account she did nothing of the sort, immersing herself instead in a tourist guide to the region while the chauffeur, blissfully ignorant of what he had just missed, became absorbed in the Arts and Leisure pages of the *Sunday Standard*.

Trusting the map provided by his informants, Personnettaz headed toward the club annex that housed the short-term guests. His equipment weighed a bit too much in his pockets, but still they didn't bulge: miniature flashlight and ring of keys in the left one; in the right (just in case) a small pistol. He met no one on his way to the annex door, crossed the foyer to the waiting elevator, and entered. This time, for the less than a minute the climb lasted, he studied himself in the mirror that filled the back of the car.

It's in elevator mirrors that you can look most exhausted. And it doesn't matter which direction it's going: whether up or down, your self-image always plummets. You worry, you wonder why, what did you do the night before to deserve this? But you needn't be alarmed, it's only an effect of the overhead bulb. It's that dull, vertical glow that makes the face earthen, deepens wrinkles and draws features, swells the bags under your eyes. Under that low-angled light, the mirror multiplies your unhealthy pallor at the speed of the elevator. It is essentially, therefore, an illusion. But Personnettaz is not aware of this. My god, I've gotten old, he thinks. I never thought it could happen. We might wonder if it isn't Donatienne's presence that is pushing this man, normally so careless of his appearance, to question the mirror this way. We might wonder if he is conscious of that possibility. We might just as easily not give a tinker's damn.

He pushed open the elevator grate: still not a living soul up and down the hallway, which he followed on tip-toe to apartment 32.

Gently he knocked on the door several times, getting no answer. After two lateral glances like a ground squirrel, he delicately gripped the knob, turning it silently. Expecting it to resist, he had selected in advance the appropriate passkey from his ring; but after barely a quarter of a turn the door opened as if on its own. Thrusting a hand in his pocket, Personnettaz closed it (just in case) over the small pistol.

Crossing first through an opaque anteroom, with no other furnishings than two disused clothes hooks on the wall, Personnettaz then entered a large, empty living room. Curtains drawn, furniture arranged, not a single trace of occupancy. A door to the right probably led to a bedroom: indeed; also empty. The man spun around pensively: nothing, at least not a personal belonging in sight. He inspected the shelving, the drawers, the wastebaskets, without finding a matchbox or hairpin, nor a single bill or flyer or crumpled ticket such as people always leave behind in hotels. No cigarette butts in the spotless ashtrays. He opened the numerous closets with no greater success— except for the last one in which rested, folded on the bottom shelf, all the fabrics bought in the afternoons by Gloire when she had nothing better to do. Personnettaz opened them one after the other, without discovering the slightest clue between their layers. Absolutely nothing. Under the influence of spite, he suddenly got the urge to rip one of those fabrics to shreds; and then, under a less precise influence, he thought of bringing one to Donatienne. But in the end he rebuffed both these impulses.

Knowing in advance that he would find not even a hair, his examination of the bathroom was purely for form's sake. He returned to the living room. The silence was absolute, although pockmarked by a distant rumble that multiplied it still more. Evidently the apartment had been emptied with care, but very recently, it seemed, for in it still floated a few nearby echoes of perfume, words, sighs, and the clack of high heels.

A cough sounded behind Personnettaz, who turned his head: a bellboy equipped with a swab and pail was studying him with interest, asking a question that Personnettaz had him repeat. The bellboy wanted to know if he could clean. Personnettaz deemed the place to be quite clean enough already. "Of course," he said nonetheless, "go ahead. In any case, I was just leaving."

In the rear of the Ambassador, Donatienne had dozed off, and on his steering wheel the native chauffeur was asleep as well—a fairly intimate twin slumber which lets us imagine that the young woman might have had second thoughts. But this hypothesis did not cross Personnettaz's mind as he lightly touched Donatienne's shoulder. When she opened her eyes: "Well," he said, "I think it's a bust."

CHAPTER 20

FROM ANOTHER XEROX-TELEX-FAX OFFICE near the Cosmopolitan Club, Donatienne called Salvador the following morning at around nine o'clock. The eighty-five degrees already weighing on the city jumped to 120 in the glass cage with its zinc roof. Donatienne immediately became drenched, while somewhere in the distance, Paris floated in icy darkness, at the hour when late night prepares to change into its early morning garb. No doubt Salvador would still be asleep, but the young woman had no qualms about waking him. And anyway, no, he was not asleep. He hadn't even gone to bed.

High as a kite, Salvador was experiencing some difficulty merely in staying seated at his table, holding on with both hands to the edge of that document-littered surface. Before his eyes, on a large blotter stained with the traces of numerous glasses—interlacings of circumferences that sketched out a dead-drunk version of the Olympic emblem —a few words were jotted in an unsteady hand: the adjectives *brunette* and *blonde* one above the other, then the nouns *cigarettes* and *beer* correspondingly superimposed across from them, with a complicated network of arrows and brackets linking the two columns. In the upper-right-hand corner of the blotter was inscribed the single word *redheads*, in parentheses and followed by a question mark. To all appearances, Salvador's research marked an idle pause that was still more idle than usual. A transistor radio set on a corner of the table broadcast, almost imperceptibly, a continuous program of tropical music.

"Ah," stammered Salvador when he answered the phone, "it's you. Great timing, I was getting kind of lonely here. Where are you? You want to come over?"

Donatienne raised her eyes to heaven.

"Listen," she said, "we blew it again. I swear, it's really something that we can't get our hands on that girl."

"Yeah," Salvador said pastily, "who cares? Nobody gives a damn. Come over."

"Don't be an idiot," Donatienne cried. "Stop it. I'm almost four thousand miles away, I'm dying of the heat, and I'm fed up, you hear?"

"Oh, right, right," said Salvador, apparently not hearing, removing the receiver from his ear for an instant to remedy his empty glass. "Me too," he resumed, "I'm fed up too, you know? More than fed up. That's putting it mildly, more than fed up."

"All right," Donatienne calmed down. "But are you getting some work done? Are you making progress?"

"Man, I'm not making anything," went Salvador. "I'm drawing blanks but I don't give a damn. I don't give a damn, you understand?" he repeated with enthusiasm. "You sure you don't want to come over?"

"No," the young woman sighed, "not right now. I'll call you later."

"Wait, wait a minute," Salvador insisted into the night —well after Donatienne had hung up, left the cabin, and rejoined Personnettaz in the Ambassador.

"So," inquired Personnettaz, "what did he say?"

"Nothing," said the young woman. "He doesn't seem to be doing too well. Where the hell could that bitch have gone to now?" she wondered through clenched teeth.

Naively, that bitch thought they would leave her in peace once she had accomplished her mission. She had arrived in Bombay and taken a room at the Supreme Hotel, where her accommodations were elementary: neither air conditioner nor television, a cement bathroom, a hard leatherette sofa, a single chair, a single table, in a drawer of which Gloire stashed the package given her by Gopal—a painstakingly Scotch-taped package, in the shape of a brick but soft in consistency, as if it contained water, pharmaceutical jelly, or air—before dialing the number the doctor had jotted on a scrap of prescription pad (V. R. Moopanar, 2021947). They apparently had not replaced the telephone since the days of the English; its dial turned with the irritating slowness of a gassed roach. But finally it rang at the other end of the line; someone picked up.

It must have been a huge enterprise for, after Gloire had asked to speak to Mr. Moopanar, a high-pitched operator's voice first advised her to hold the wire. Click. Another female voice, more contralto this time, same request and same advice, another click. Then the uneasy tones of a circumspect young man: double click, after which an older, calmer man, no doubt sitting in a more comfortable chair, desired more information: first name, last name, who referred you? He, too, advised her to hold the wire when Gloire mentioned the name Gopal. Triple click followed by a buzz. Another female voice, more commanding this time, clipped, executive secretary–style: double buzz. More comfortable and jovial, the last voice finally seemed to be that of V. R. Moopanar himself.

"Ah, Gopal," Moopanar exclaimed, "I see exactly who you mean. Now let's see, is he the one in Hyderabad or the one on TTK Road?"

"Goodness," said Gloire, "I don't really know. He's got a clinic on Karaneeswarar Sannadhi Street."

"Perfect," the other cut in, "I see exactly. Where are you staying? The Supreme, ah, well, are you sure you're comfortable there? Well, anyway, we'll meet at the bar, all right? I'm on my way. We're on our way."

He appeared thirty minutes later. Talcumed, ringed, mustache waxed, replete in his raspberry double-breasted suit, Moopanar smiled, smiled, smiled. Each time he smiled, a diamond embedded in one of his canines rang like an electric pinball bumper. Flanking him in the background, his inverse, was a dry, clean-shaven young man squeezed into tight-fitting chocolate brown and suffering from a peculiar strabismus: a killer's steady left eye, a bodyguard's very mobile right one. While he showed only minor interest in Gopal's parcel, not even glancing at it as he passed it to his assistant, Moopanar proved very affable with Gloire, hoped she'd had a good trip, wasn't too tired, welcome to Bombay. Did she know anyone in town, wouldn't she be too alone, wasn't she going to get bored. Unthinkable that she should be bored: might he have the honor of inviting her to a party that he happened to be throwing that very evening, at home? A few friends. A chance to meet people and make friends. His diamond rang four times, followed by the sharp explosion of a free game, as he stressed all the advantages of having friends in Bombay. "I'm not sure," said Gloire. "The fact is, I'm pretty worn out."

"That's only natural," said Moopanar, "I'll let you get some rest. I'll call you toward the end of the afternoon. A car can come by to pick you up."

Back in her room, Gloire consulted Beliard: what

should I do? "Why not go," suggested the homunculus. "You never know. What's there to lose? After that, we'll see."

Moopanar occupied the penthouse of a deluxe residence in Malabar Hill. Depending on which end of the terrace one stood at, one's gaze plummeted onto the Gulf of Oman, the bay, the launderers' quarter, or hanging gardens. Tables had been set, laden with enough to souse and stuff two hundred people, though there were but a mere sixty: V. R. Moopanar's immediate entourage. First, all his mistresses and all his brothers and all the brothers of his mistresses and all the mistresses of his brothers. Then Moopanar's colleagues, who seemed to be accompanied by their attendants; certain industrialists; a vice minister; a Congress Party deputy; three Hungarian businessmen without their spouses; and five or six prostitutes. Finally, a few racing professionals—owners, trainers, jockeys. Mixed Western and regional outfits, tuxes and shawls, tailored suits, saris, pajamas and miniskirts, turbans, and pantsuits; no pinky without its gem.

Warmly introduced by Moopanar, Gloire mingled with a few groups, smiling and saying little, feigning not to know English, seeming absent from the conversations. Although all around her they were discussing business rather freely, she had some trouble getting a precise idea of these people's occupations. Then she ended up growing bored: drink in hand, she left the terrace to go tour the apartment.

A wide hallway bordered numerous rooms with brightly painted walls. Through their open doorways, Gloire inspected them one after the other, like a catalogue of sherbets. The floor of each was tiled in matching marble tones, waxed like hardwood, so polished it could be mistaken for linoleum. These rooms were for the most part furnished only with a large bed, a large chandelier, and a large Cuddalore or Masulipatam carpet, or sometimes with a tiger skin still bearing its head and all its teeth. The door to one room was partially closed: Gloire pushed it open before immediately shutting it, having had time only to glimpse a couple writhing on a bed. She walked away, disturbed, then doubly disturbed when she realized that one of the faces of that couple, barely seen, might not be unknown to her. She stopped, retraced her steps, gently opened the door again, and didn't recognize Rachel until the latter began crying out *yes do it up the ass, Biplab, please you know you like it*. "Well, I'll be damned," Gloire said to herself. "She's still with Biplab."

It was so unexpected that Gloire, against all her principles, remained frozen at the door without being able to look away—until Rachel, acting on her word and flopping over on the bed, met her stare and cried out once more in a different tone. Gloire, mortified, immediately turned and left. But she had gone no more than a few yards down the hall when, bare feet slapping the marble, Rachel ran up to her, hastily wrapped in a cotton bathrobe. "What are you *doing* here?"

"It's kind of a long story," answered Gloire. "What about you?"

If Rachel hadn't changed much in such a short time, her life on the other hand had been completely transformed. Tired of traveling without goal or method, she had as we know become involved with the young businessman Biplab, whom she'd met near the Elephanta wharf. Now Biplab, newly recruited in the Moopanar company and quickly risen in the ranks, ensured her an easy life in Bombay, one of unadulterated idleness and royal peace. "He's sweet," she said, "and besides, you know, him or someone else."

"I see," said Gloire. "But what is this company, exactly?"

"What," went Rachel, "you haven't figured it out yet?"

At the end of the hall, wearing new clothes and a wide smile, the young businessman appeared and came toward Rachel, obviously head over heels in love. "Go have a drink on the terrace," she told him. "I'll join you in a minute."

From what she had understood of Gopal's activities, Gloire had expected to meet his counterparts in Bombay, involved like him in the traffic of narcotics and blood. But actually, explained Rachel, these two markets conglutinated into a much larger and more developed network, of which the Moopanar company was one of the nerve centers. From this consortium of various businesses, which constituted an alternative global economy (or perhaps the globe's one true economy), Rachel drew up a table with three headings: goods, services, methods.

The goods: classic commodities, first and foremost, including military explosives, heavy weaponry, currency, alcohol, children, cigarettes, pornographic materials, counterfeit, slaves of both sexes, endangered species. On top of which, new sectors had recently begun to expand rapidly. Human organs, for example—kidneys and corneas lifted from Eastern European battlefields, in the quack clinics of Central America or the subcontinent, more or less healthy blood pumped pretty much everywhere—constituted no less active a market than the one for radioactive products left over from the dismantled nuclear plants in the East: uranium, cesium, and strontium by the shovelful, plutonium like rainwater.

Gigantic poppies, moreover, with miraculous yields, were springing up at top speed around those deboned power plants, helping feed the traditional market for narcotics, another speciality of the Moopanar company. Add some twenty thousand brands of bogus pharmaceuticals, and you've got something that produced masses of good narcodollars and excellent narcomarks, all indispensable for maintaining a voluminous staff of chemists, recyclers, and hired killers.

For the services: The hired killers also contributed their share of rackets and kidnappings, including ransom, extortion, protection money, gambling, and prostitution, redirecting of development grants, misappropriation of international aid or community funds, secret accounts or moonlight labor, investment scams, disposal of toxic waste, forced subcontracts, illicit bankruptcies, and agricultural policy fraud—a whole world, in short.

Yes, the world is teeming with things to do, and for anyone who knows how to do them methodically it is teeming with money. This money is gathered by collectors wearing light-colored ties over dark shirts; then laundered by an arborescence of casinos and palaces, pizzerias and hair salons, massage parlors, coin-op laundries, and service stations; then wired into untouchable accounts in Bad Ischl, Székesfehérvár, or the Anglo-Norman islands. But Gloire had pretty much read all this in the newspapers; she began to grow tired of these explanations. For now, she preferred to take Rachel in her arms.

"All right," she whispered softly in her ear, "but tell me, what am I doing here?"

"They'll let you know soon enough," Rachel answered through Gloire's hair, "it won't be long. Come."

They went back into the room, Rachel closing the door more carefully this time, and fell onto the bed. And a few hours later, back at the Supreme, Gloire gave Beliard a rundown of her evening, minus a few technical details.

"I see what the deal is," said the homunculus, "and I know you're having fun. Even so, be careful. Maybe we shouldn't hang around here too long."

CHAPTER 21

THE DAY AFTER HIS PARTY, Moopanar phoned the Supreme to inform Gloire that he'd found her another hotel, better suited to her person. A car would be by before noon to fetch her and her belongings. "The plot thickens," Beliard observed.

The glacial darkness of the restaurant, the bouncers dressed as trainers and the elevator boys as ichoglans, gave a fair idea of this new establishment's prestige. Located on the top floor of a white building rising high above Marine Drive, Gloire's new room was six times larger than at the Supreme, decorated in dark colors and endowed with every modern comfort—refrigerator, television, air conditioner, and bathtub for two. A small balcony overhanging the void supported a lounge chair and a bay window that looked out onto the bay.

Gloire quickly resumed her old habits. Rising late, she spent the ends of her mornings on the balcony, eyes half-closed on the vast and sparsely populated beach strewn with decrepit attractions, rusted slides, and turnstiles. The unclean sea was far away, the sand was only dust. Passers-by trampled it in isolation, with no intention of bathing, sometimes behind an ox cart. Occasionally one could see a horse in the background, galloping over the fringe of sea foam. Lying as usual on the lounge's footrest and wearing only his Bermuda shorts, Beliard soaked up the sun next to Gloire. "Be careful even so," he advised. "Don't let yourself become indebted to them. Don't let them get a hold over you. Insist on paying for the hotel yourself."

Moopanar, however, was very discreet. He called briefly from time to time to make sure that Gloire wanted for nothing, without imposing or even proposing anything—except that she grace the parties he continued to throw on his terrace two or three times a week. These parties were always generally the same; Gloire ended up going only every other time. One day she agreed to accompany Moopanar, with Rachel, to the racetrack where one of his horses, named Telepathy, was running at four to one. Two days later, they watched a polo match that pitted other members of his stables against each other.

But for the time being: sun. Then, at around two o'clock, Rachel would rap softly at the door. "Scram," Gloire would tell Beliard, who slunk off with the sullen eye of a dispossessed voyeur. Sometimes he got up of his own accord as soon as he heard the knock, not waiting for Gloire to kick him out but making a sour face all the same. The young women rested a moment in the room before going to have a leisurely lunch at the hotel restaurant—cubes of marinated chicken and fish, yogurt with bhang. Then, once the worst heat had passed, they went back to galavanting about town as in the old days, near the Chor Bazar or the Banganga Tank, loitering around the reservoirs in the shadows of tall buildings. Monkeys, men, and children played on the roof terraces. Men waving handkerchiefs guided the movements of pigeons grouped in clusters in the sky, the children governed those of their kites, and the monkeys chased each other around the sheer drops of the facades; you never saw any women playing.

When night fell, they dined at the Yacht Club, where Biplab sometimes joined them before going off to resume his functions at Moopanar's. Then, almost as gay as that first evening, they went to down a few glasses at the bar of the Taj, which was still full of foreigners, meeting other young women there—one of whom swore, one evening, that she answered to the name of Porsche Duvall—as well as men and boys. The men were moodier and more forward than the boys, with whom it was easier to negotiate, although the women seemed to have an equal number of friends and enemies in both camps. In short, hardly a care, easy life, royal peace. Gloire didn't even have to fear the maneuvers of Personnettaz and company; Gopal had covered her tracks so well that for the moment they'd lost all trace of her.

Still, it would sometimes happen that she could no longer find her equilibrium, no longer hear herself in the incessant concert of car horns and crows in Bombay—as had been the case, albeit in reverse, when her thoughts stood out too violently in the oppressive quiet of the Cosmopolitan Club. It also happened that she began wondering if she was going to stay there indefinitely, if it wasn't time to go home. On that score, Rachel couldn't answer, Beliard had no opinion, and I myself don't really know. Whatever the case, after three weeks of this diet, Moopanar showed up at Gloire's one morning, unexpectedly: Beliard barely had time to jump into a closet.

Moopanar at first claimed that, having been in the neighborhood, he'd suddenly thought of dropping by just to make sure all was well. He crossed the room, contemplated the bay for a moment, then turned toward Gloire: "Could you do me a small favor?"

"Here we go," a breathless Beliard said to himself, ear glued to the closet door in the darkness.

"What sort of favor?"

"It's very simple," said Moopanar. "I have to send some merchandise to your country. You'd merely have to accompany that merchandise. Make sure everything goes smoothly. Be there, in other words."

"The plot thickens," Beliard repeated under his breath.

Gloire didn't answer right away. It might be an opportunity to go home, as she'd been thinking of doing lately —but, knowing Moopanar's activities, at what cost, with who knew what blocks of plastique, uranium, or opium stuffed into which private place?

"Please don't go imagining things," Moopanar read her thoughts. "There's nothing complicated, nothing risky. All you have to do is take a plane. I'll assume all expenses, there's nothing you have to do. Someone will be waiting for you over there to handle everything."

"Fine," said Gloire, "let's assume that's true. And what exactly is it you're transporting?"

"Horses," said Moopanar.

"Oh, really," said Gloire. "Horses."

"Yes," said Moopanar, "horses."

"Well, in that case," said Gloire, "if it's only horses."

"Horses," repeated Moopanar. "So you see. Only horses."

Cargo planes were what one used to transport horses from one continent to another. Normally a veterinarian would escort them, armed with a giant syringe in case there was a problem, but, Moopanar assured her, there would be no problems so there would be no veterinarian; Gloire could travel alone with the animals. The day after tomorrow. All right? "All right," she said.

So: Bombay–Saha Airport, the day after tomorrow. Bright sunshine, moderate wind from the northeast. Apart from Moopanar's six horses—of an old Central Asian lineage —the cargo plane would carry the turbine shaft for a hydraulic dam, sent back to France for routine replace-ment. The whole interior of the plane had been gutted, reduced to the state of an immense hold, with only a win-dowless cabin installed behind the pilot's cockpit for the escorts. It had six seats in front, along with a microwave oven and a freezer compartment. One door permitted access to the cockpit, another led to a steel stairway that descended into the hold. A steward out of uniform provided limited service. Gloire kissed Rachel and they took off.

Three men in civvies were escorting the turbine shaft, young technicians specializing in the maintenance of enor-mous things. Three young men in fine fettle and very talk-ative among themselves, but too bashful to dare speak to Gloire, who distractedly heard them launch into a thousand topics. But it seemed that on each of these topics their con-versation, at first quite animated, rapidly petered out before frankly spinning in idle: after the first light, lively, dancing exchanges, it soon got stuck in a rut. Then they would clam-ber off to dig it out, unfold their collapsible shovels, and stuff branches under the wheels—after which, as soon as it was lifting off and airborne once more, soaring toward another topic, they would jump aboard the conversation at the last second, before it could fly away without them.

Gloire followed their exchange for a moment before dozing off. When she opened her eyes, the technicians were asleep. As usual on a plane, Beliard was unavailable, not even visible: no one to talk to, nothing to see out the nonexistent windows, nothing to read; Gloire was starting to get bored. As luck would have it, the copilot soon appeared, en route to the refrigerator to get something to drink. Seeing her with nothing to do, he invited her to come have one with him and the others in the cockpit. He grabbed a bottle and stepped aside to let her pass.

Equally calm ambience in the pilots' cabin. The captain

was asleep in his seat and the flight engineer was leafing through specialized magazines. "Good evening, gentlemen," said Gloire. The captain smiled as he opened a blue eye: his jaws were square and his crew cut white. "I've got the corkscrew," the engineer reminded them. Having settled the young woman in a seat behind the staff, the copilot regained his position before the automatic maneuver dials. The captain sat up in his chair—the back of which was lined with a curtain of ergonomic pearls, of the same model used by taxi drivers with delicate lumbars—then turned toward Gloire. They were flying over Saudi Arabia.

Paris–Charles de Gaulle Airport, three hours later. Cool, drizzle. Gloire left the Boeing with the crew, who went to their reserved quarters to shower and change before heading home while she would go through customs alone with the horses' papers. She calmly handled all the formalities. The documents seemed to be in order; they stamped everything they could stamp. She was told where she could claim her cargo. To do that, she had to leave the terminal and go to a freight hangar. Moopanar had indeed mentioned that someone would be waiting for her in Paris to take care of everything, but if this someone didn't show, what would she do all alone in life with six horses? We'd see.

We see. Barely past the opaque door amid travelers arriving on other flights, among the relatives and allies come to meet them, we spot a face whose mobility made it stand out from all the others. Still devoured by facial tics, but in a more minor key than usual: Lagrange.

"Hey!" said Gloire. "What are you doing here?"

"I'll explain," said Lagrange. He seemed to be in a very bad mood.

"You seem to be in a very bad mood," Gloire observed.

"You're right," Lagrange admitted. "I'm in a very bad mood."

An associate was with him, someone Gloire had never met. Jockey's build, dark clothes, a gap between his incisors that could fit a molar and answering to the name Zbigniew, he coordinated the three vans in which the horses would embark. They waited for the latter, which appeared in the distance. The animals shivered, gave indolent kicks, seemed not very lively, whereas Lagrange showed signs of increasing nervousness all during the transfer. And yet nothing particular caught the attention of the customs functionaries. The final papers, in order like the rest, were stamped.

Normally they send dogs, cats, and monkeys through the X-rays; with no special care they toss their carriers onto the luggage belt with the inanimate valises. But they didn't have any machines big enough to scan the horses, which paraded, in step, from the airplane into the vans. Gloire hadn't seen them when she embarked in Bombay, nor had she gone down to visit them in the hold. Fairly dazed, rings under their eyes, bloated, they did everything they were told; only distantly did they evoke steeplechases and polo matches. Having locked the rear gates, the associate walked back toward Lagrange, wiping his hands: "All set," he said. "Nice animals."

"Right," said Lagrange, "get moving. I'll see you Thursday. You and I" (to Gloire) "are taking a cab."

They watched the vans drive off, then headed for the taxi stand.

"So," intimated Lagrange, "how did it go with Moopanar?"

As Gloire stopped short, Lagrange took two more steps, then turned around.

"What?" he said. "Come on, let's go."

"Wait a minute," she said. "You know that guy? You work with those people?"

"Come on," said Lagrange. "I'll explain."

They joined the taxi line, but these vehicles were scarce

for the moment. By the time they had found the only available one and climbed inside, the flight captain had come running up in freshly pressed civilian garb. Knocking on their window, the captain asked if they wouldn't possibly mind taking him along. "Of course," said Gloire, while Lagrange turned away without answering.

The captain sat next to the driver, sighing contentedly. "This is very kind of you," he said. "You can just let me off at Place d'Italie."

At the wheel was a classic French taxi driver in black and white, yellow cigarette stub, wiseguy accent, checkered cap. "Ah," sympathized the captain, "I see you've got one of those beaded seats too."

"Lemme tell you," said the driver, "this thing saved my life."

"It's remarkable," said the captain, "simply remarkable how relaxing it is."

"It's some kinda Chinese thing," said the driver, "right?"

"I'm not entirely sure," said the captain, "maybe Scandinavian. But how good it feels, how good it does feel."

"Me," said the driver, "I used to get a stiff back like you wouldn't believe."

"Why, so did I," the captain hastened to concur. "But I think that's Place d'Italie now."

"So," said Gloire as soon as he had gotten out, "how are you mixed up in all this?"

"I'll explain," said Lagrange, "but first tell me where you want to go."

"Anywhere," answered Gloire, "so long as I'm left in peace."

"What would you say to the country?" Lagrange suggested.

"Fine," said Gloire.

"Perfect," said Lagrange.

CHAPTER 22

THEY WENT TO THE COUNTRY. Lagrange didn't explain squat.

After the taxi dropped them on Rue de Tilsitt, they immediately left for Normandy in Lagrange's Opel; he remained mute on the highway, then on the smaller roads they took after it. They wound through a copse for three quarters of an hour. At a bend in a single-lane filiform drive, a wrought-iron gate opened onto a prospect of lindens at the end of which stood a small manor in pink brick. They weren't very far from the sea, past Honfleur, somewhere around Manneville-la-Raoult.

They arrived just after noon. Built in the late seventeenth century, the manor stood drily against the yellowed prairies: a tall, brittle parallelepiped, thin and almost transparent. Large windows symmetrically cut in its facades let light pass through from one side to the other. Kitchen and living rooms on the ground floor, and two other floors filled with bedrooms.

The room he gave Gloire occupied the entire top floor. The exposed beams made it look like a capsized boat; the windows were of irregular unrefined glass, lightly tinted, containing small bubbles that distorted the landscape. Antique furniture, modern paintings, and figurines— among which, four miles in the distance, was the spanking new Normandy bridge framed by one of the six windows, a perfect little contemporary sculpture impeccably lit in its showcase.

The young woman looked out the other windows. To one side of the narrow road at the end of the park, a low, whitewashed building in traditional style, with iris stalks on a fringe of thatch, must have served as toolshed and lodgings for the staff. On the other side, beyond a garden, a tennis court with a sagging net, and a tarpaulin-covered pool, horses stood planted in a field. Lagrange and Zbigniew were watching them, their elbows resting on the fence. Gloire went down to join the two men.

The animals numbered around ten and moved little. Three of them nodded their heads together in a corner; two colts wandered around their mother; and the others posed for their statues. Gloire did not recognize Moopanar's horses among them, seen that very morning at the airport. No doubt they were recovering from their journey in the complex of stables and individual stalls framing a bridle path at the other end of the field. They already looked fairly languid as they got off the plane to walk into the van, without fuss or hurry, without anyone suspecting that the first three of them were carrying sixty grams of cesium each and the other three had five kilos of heroin, the latter in plastic wrapping and the former in lead containers. Yes, no doubt they were recuperating after they had had the loads extracted from their entrails, before being brought to conclude this piece of business at the knacker's yard.

"Horses are pretty enormous," Zbigniew pointed out. "You can put all kinds of things inside."

"Shut up already," said Lagrange.

He himself would continue to remain silent for the rest of the day, then the next day; he no longer seemed the same person. In the six weeks Gloire had been gone, Lagrange had changed, and so had the days, now getting longer and longer: the sky was wider, the colors more sustained. And the season, growing milder, must have inspired lighter thoughts, since fairly late on the third night, after the last news broadcast, Lagrange, after having drunk a fair amount downstairs by himself, tried to join Gloire in her room. "No," Gloire said through the door. Lagrange took a clumsy stab at forcing the lock but gave up almost immediately; his unsteady footfalls faded down the stairway.

"What, is he kidding?" Beliard muttered, rolling over under the bedspread. "That's all we needed." The next morning, the sky was black as if the sun didn't want to rise, or as if night had rebelled and refused to give way: here I am and here I stay, you won't get rid of me that easily.

The darkness was more accommodating above Paris, yielding to the daylight at around six in the morning over Place de la République, and finally moving off to get on with its life. On the fourth floor of a building on Rue Yves-Toudic, behind République, Personnettaz had stopped sleeping some time ago. He finally got up, went into the kitchen, and poured two tablespoons of instant coffee into a mug. He opened the hot water faucet, let it run until it was good and hot, tested the stream with a rapid finger to make sure, then filled the mug, which he carried back unsweetened to his room. He sat down at his table and drank this bitter potion in little sips, while reading Jack London's adventures in the gold country. Forty minutes later his radio alarm went off in the middle of a sentence about the Dow Jones, and Personnettaz cut off the next one, devoted to the Nikkei average, before closing his book.

The sound of the shut tome echoed briefly in the room and the man headed, alone, to the bathroom. "You shouldn't keep living all alone like that," the concierge of his building had advised him once upon a time. "Someday you'll be old and sick with no one to take care of you."

The bearer of a Yugoslavian passport, the concierge back then was an elderly man, meticulously dressed, who would bring up the mail every day in pearl-colored suit and purple tie. But that was several years ago. Since then, a fair number of things had changed. Tenants had come and gone, Personnettaz had moved one floor down, and the management had repossessed the concierge's lodge to convert it into a studio, so there was no longer a concierge nor, for that matter, a Yugoslavia; but Personnettaz, despite the advice, persisted in living all alone like that. Chances not to live alone had presented themselves, of course, but he hadn't seized them, and now they were presenting themselves less often, less and less often. There would probably be no one to share with Personnettaz the tail end of an inheritance, seasoned with obscure bonds in manganese or zinc or cadmium, very far away, that he owned from he hardly knew where.

Little supplementary revenues sporadically came in from the operations proposed by Jouve, but on that score Personnettaz found himself technically laid off for the moment. All trace of Gloire had been lost since the attempt in India, and Donatienne had returned to Stochastic. While basically relieved to be rid of her, Personnettaz still phoned Donatienne from time to time, to take stock of the situation.

He threw on a few things without noticing whether they matched, vaguely promising himself to buy some new shoes one of these days—this pair easily had forty thousand on the odometer. But apart from that prospect, there was nothing else to do today; no more or less than yesterday.

And nothing can wear you down like idleness when you live in an opaque two-room apartment behind République.

He waited until nine o'clock to make two or three phone calls. First to Boccara, but in vain. Daily since his return, Personnettaz had tried without success to reach the young man. On the off chance he had even stopped by his place but, once in front of the building, he hadn't been able to remember the new door code; he had only a mnemonic recall of the old one. Boccara indeed seemed not to have returned from his cruise, and so Personnettaz dialed Jouve's number. But, once more on the verge of tears from reading a sentimental novel, Mrs. Jouve answered that Jouve was out, as he was so often, as he was increasingly often. Perhaps he would be back tomorrow. Personnettaz announced his visit for the following afternoon. Then he called Salvador.

Nothing new at Stochastic, either, and Salvador's voice was somewhat less than affable. Personnettaz informed him of his plan to visit Jouve, which served no other purpose than to make him appear active. "Fine," Salvador said with scant enthusiasm. "Well, keep me posted. Ah, I think Donatienne wants to talk to you—I'll put her on."

"No," Personnettaz blurted too late, "no."

"What's this I hear?" said Donatienne. "You're seeing Jouve tomorrow? I'm coming with you."

"There's no point," said Personnettaz. "I really think there's no point. I can handle it perfectly well on my own."

"No," Donatienne said gravely, "you need me and you know it. I'll see you tomorrow."

She sits back down in front of her keyboard, laughing to herself, waiting for the other one to start dictating again; but for the moment the other one is silent. He sits quietly. His face is blank. He is reflecting. He's demoralized. He has come to work on foot from Place de la Nation.

Walking by the base of one of the columns that embellish that square, the thought of finding himself one hundred feet above ground level, in the place of Philippe Auguste, brutally rekindled his vertigo. Right now he's on the verge of nausea.

Then Salvador stops bothering even to reflect. He ponders a midge, come from who knows where, that circulates around his desk, also on foot, peacefully skirting the computer and the pencil can, slaloming between the floppy disks, the mineral water, and the bottle of aspirin. Coming and going among these accessories, the midge sometimes pauses more lengthily before one of them, seems to look it over, takes a few steps back and then heads off again, a tourist among the monuments. The contemplation of that insect inspires a few consoling thoughts in Salvador's brain: this isn't so bad, I could have ended up in Manila selling cigarettes one by one. He goes back to his reflections. "Let's continue," he says. "Take this down. Warm tall blondes and cool tall blondes, part two."

So alongside warm blondes, there also exist cool tall blondes with measured words, radiographic eyes, and strict tailored suits. They are perhaps more distinguished, more civilized than the warm tall blondes, but the world, for opposite reasons, fears them just the same. At best, lunar, they stiffen in its arms; at worst they evaporate out of them. They run the risk of transparency, expose themselves to the danger of chlorosis. They are seldom light-hearted. Eva Marie-Saint is fairly typical of the genre. There is also a bit of this with Ingrid Bergman, for example.

"How about Grace Kelly?" suggests Donatienne.

"Absolutely," says Salvador, "absolutely. You have some of that with Grace Kelly. Now we're getting somewhere."

CHAPTER 23

HER SENTIMENTAL NOVEL RESTING ON HER KNEES, Mrs. Jouve is sitting very stiffly on the edge of the sofa, alone before her television, which at this hour of the afternoon broadcasts only series produced across the Atlantic or beyond the Rhine. Acted by siliconed actresses with hairdos sculpted from a solid block, laquered and thermoset, the series are also sentimental. So that, regardless of whether she's following the plot on the page or on the screen, regardless of whether she takes off or puts on her glasses, behind them or not Mrs. Jouve's tears are still flowing. She is awaiting the return of her husband. She has not cleaned house very thoroughly: the remains of her lunch lie scattered on the table; on the bed in the next room the sheets are still rumpled.

Rattle of keys in the foyer and Jouve appears, his briefcase dangling at the end of his arm. Entering the living room, the reddened eyes of his spouse make him avert his own and roll them upward. "You can't imagine what kind of day I've had," he claims, listing the succession of obstacles and meetings purported to have eaten away his time.

"I'm not asking for an account," his wife answers in a tearful voice.

"But I'm just telling you things, Genevieve," Jouve says gently, "that's all. I just want you to know everything."

He opens his briefcase and rummages inside, looking for nothing in particular. He considers himself above suspicion. No perfume emanates from him; his collar isn't stained with red, nor is his hair too freshly combed: Jouve is pretty well organized. Even if it happens that too great an absence of clues only connotes guilt all the more. The proof: "All you ever do is screw other women," Mrs. Jouve observes painfully.

"Hey, there, Genevieve," Jouve objects, "first of all, I don't only screw other women, all right?" Then, turning toward the half-open door to their room: "You could have cleaned up a little, don't you think? Straightened things up a bit, no?"

"I am who I am," Mrs. Jouve concedes. "I'm sure *they're* more fun to be around."

"Now, Genevieve," Jouve protests, "whatever have you cooked up in that head of yours?"

She turns away when he attempts a small gesture of affection. Changing the subject, Genevieve Jouve is about to tell him about Personnettaz's visit when the doorbell rings and there he is, followed by Donatienne, who is more skimpily clad than ever. If that way of dressing puts Personnettaz ill at ease, Jouve's roving eye, on the other hand, is interested.

While Genevieve Jouve talks with Donatienne, Personnettaz takes Jouve aside. It's inconceivable that a simple matter such as Gloire's shouldn't be easily resolved. It's unbelievable that they don't have a single remaining lead. Just find him one tiny clue and Personnettaz guarantees he'll be back on the case, he'll wrap it up in no time.

Personnettaz does not like the constant delays in this operation, nor the feeling of incompetence that he gets from them, nor the enforced idleness that derives from them. It seems to have become a personal issue with him.

Jouve listens while appearing to think, but his eyes continue to glide furtively toward Donatienne. Surreptitiously they divest the young woman of her light textile wrapping. "Fine, I'll see," he finally says. "I'll see what I can do."

Meanwhile, Mrs. Jouve and Donatienne exchange female viewpoints on mostly female subjects, but not exclusively, not exclusively. Turning toward them, Personnettaz notes that Donatienne seems to be getting along very well with Genevieve Jouve. Personnettaz has known his employer's wife for a long time; he feels more comfortable with her than with him. That she should enjoy the young woman's company suddenly seems to him to constitute an agreement, a guarantee, a sanction. In emotional matters, Personnettaz has a pathological need for third-party approval. For the first time he looks at Donatienne differently, but just for a moment. Then he glances at his watch and Jouve, by contagion, looks at his own and, following suit, Donatienne and Genevieve similarly consult theirs. Everyone in fact is wearing a watch; each of them, on the occasion of an exam, a birthday, or a federal or religious holiday, has been handcuffed to time; all four observe, with a few seconds' difference, the same phenomenon of nearly four-twenty. Personnettaz says they'll be going. They're going.

"Did you see what she was wearing?" Genevieve asks after they've left.

"Oh, no," murmurs Jouve, "I didn't notice."

"Like hell you didn't notice," says Genevieve. "Anyway, never mind. I know what that means, when they dress like that."

"Oh, really?" Jouve perks up. "So what does it mean?"

"It's one of two things," states Genevieve. "Either there's a man they're out to attract, or they're completely desperate. But what are you doing? Are you going out again?"

"I'm going back to see your brother," says Jouve. "And believe me, it's not with a joyful heart."

This time, Jouve hails a taxi that heads up Boulevard de Sébastopol, veers in front of the Gare de l'Est, and crosses the Canal Saint-Martin before rounding the Buttes-Chaumont toward the Amérique police station. At the reception desk, the only client is an African in a suit who has a document case cut from the same synthetic fibers in the same color. This African, who would like to procure the requisite forms for a family immigration procedure— "That's right," says the functionary on duty, "bring over the whole tribe"—is sent packing in short order. Jouve goes directly up to his brother-in-law's office.

The latter grimaces disgracefully when he sees Jouve. "And what," he asks, "do you want from me now?"

"Nothing," says Jouve. "The same as last time."

"Oh no, I'm not biting anymore," says Clauze. "I have no reason to help you out."

"All right," says Jouve, opening his briefcase, "listen. I'm tired of this squabble. I'm going to make you an offer for the good of the family. Let's make up, what do you say? I've got the receipt. Here it is, you can have it back."

The receipt consists of three typewritten sheets of tea green onionskin paper stapled in one corner. Clauze grabs it and looks it over. "It feels funny to see this again," he says, shaking his head with an evil smile. "It's been a while.

"I can imagine," says Jouve, also smiling. "I understand."

Clauze leafs through the document attentively. "Hey, wait a minute," he says, "isn't there something missing here?"

"No," Jouve exclaims ingenuously. "You think so? And yet that's all I found in my files."

"You're trying to diddle me," Clauze says bitterly. "You think you're going to stick me in the back."

"I'm not!" cries Jouve. "I don't!"

"All the stuff about the meat is missing," Clauze insists, waving the document in his face.

"I don't know what you're talking about," says Jouve. "But fine, if that's how you're going to be, I'm taking it back." And with a quick motion he repossesses it.

"Wait!" says Clauze. "No, let me have it. It's something, at least."

"Uh-uh," says Jouve, "no way. If you don't trust me, then it's got to be even-steven. I'll let you have it back if you get me more information about the girl."

For a few seconds, Clauze fixes Jouve with a somewhat loveless stare. Then: "Wait here a minute," he finally says. While waiting for his brother-in-law to return, through the window Jouve watches the same branch from the other day limply waving. The same and yet different, for now it's sprouting buds. Five o'clock.

Clauze reappears more quickly than the last time, a new document in hand. Three handwritten lines on a page from an address book specify the address of a geriatric institution in the Seine-Maritime. "Here," he says, "I was able to find this. Now give me back those papers."

"Of course," says Jouve. "Here. I should give Genevieve your love, I suppose?"

"That's right," says Clauze, getting up to open the door. "You give her my love. You give her all my love and then you go straight to Hell."

"Robert," Jouve exclaims plaintively, "Robert, why do you always say that to me?"

CHAPTER 24

THE DAYS PASSED, meagerly furnished with short walks in the country (hawthorn, sunken paths, hedges, cows) or by the sea (iodine, jetties, wrack, seagulls), with the soon-wearisome observation of the horses, with inattentive readings and distracted spells in front of the television. Gloire might have taken better advantage of the fresh air, the healthy and varied food, the calm sleep with all windows open; she might have gotten some exercise; but the idea never even occurred to her.

She was finding these days very long, checked the time too often. Never had the march of time seemed so slow. A discouraging slowness, multiplied by itself, weighing at the threshold of immobility. The slowness of grass growing; the slowness of an ai, of glue. If there are words whose meaning determines their career, slowness is no doubt in the first rank: so slow that it hasn't yet found the slightest synonym for itself, whereas speed, which doesn't waste a minute, already has a ton of them.

Beliard, too, consulted his watch ceaselessly, winding it every other minute. Buckled to his wrist, that little mechanism from before the age of quartz was one of the few accessories in his size that the homunculus owned, along with a comb, a mirror, a handkerchief, and a pair of dark sunglasses. At first he had tried to continue wearing those sunglasses, as in the good old days of the warm countries; but, unable to see in the Norman light and bumping into everything, he soon had to give them up. Before long, he started showing signs of moodiness; he pouted, made scenes. He missed his beautiful vacation in the tropics, was getting bored silly, threatened to leave. "Fine, that's just fine," an exasperated Gloire said once, "get lost. Get lost already. I'm sick of you."

Beliard immediately jumped onto his soles while wagging his finger: "I forbid you to use that tone with me," he stamped. "Don't go thinking you're the first one I've ever looked after, eh? I've already advised more important people than you. Famous people. In show business and everything."

"So?" asked Gloire. "Are they dead?"

"Why should they be dead?" Beliard exploded. "I'm good at my job."

As she was expressing surprise that these important people, if they were still alive, should no longer require his services, Beliard began to pout while examining his teeth in his pocket mirror. In a muffled voice he alluded to certain past problems. He did not wish to dwell on the circumstances of his dismissals. "Excuse me," said Gloire, "what was that you said? Can you repeat that?" Grudgingly, the homunculus again mumbled the word *dismissal.* "Wait a second," said Gloire. "Do you mean to tell me you can be *fired?*"

"Of course I can," said Beliard. "You just have to want it."

"But that's what I want," said Gloire. "That's exactly what I want."

"No way," snickered Beliard, sticking out his black tongue in the circular mirror. "You don't want it enough."

"Little clown," concluded Gloire. "Pathetic little fucking clown."

In short, minor conflicts, as always happen when things drag on, and when they drag on too long, you get annoyed over nothing and everything. You get annoyed at Beliard, at Lagrange, and even at Zbigniew. At the horses. You get annoyed that a dog, which is itself being annoyed by another dog, should bark at the other end of the lawn all morning. You also get pretty bored. Like Genevieve and Jouve. And for lack of anything better you spend more and more time in front of the television. You watch movies ("You're going to lose her, Alex. She thinks she's in love with you"), you watch game shows ("And now I'm going to ask for your full attention, Roger. Which flowers does one see most often on balconies?" "Water lilies, no I mean petunias, uh no what I meant to say was geraniums." "I'm sorry, Roger, but I'll have to go with your first answer. So, water lilies"), you watch the news. They never talk about Gloire on the news; moreover, there's no reason they should. And yet she still dreads it. "You're not afraid they'll talk about you," Beliard once suggested, perniciously, "but that they won't. Hey, cut it out!" he cried the next second. "You know I can't stand physical violence."

And so, free of danger but also of future prospects, twelve interminable days passed, not at all as Gloire had envisioned them—sheltered, certainly, but cramped. One evening she tried to get to know Zbigniew, except that Zbigniew didn't really have a lot to say for himself. She had quickly run through the few books lining the shelves in the living room. Beliard continued to sulk, and Lagrange was now drinking every day, beginning earlier and earlier. The time had come to find something to do.

Gloire set about it one bright and sunny morning, before Lagrange got started, by asking him to drive her to Rouen. Just a quick little round trip, they'd be back for dinner. "Gee," said Lagrange, "why not? It'll be a change. Let's go." And so they took the road to Rouen. At Pont-Audemer, while Lagrange filled the Opel, Gloire walked away from the gas station toward a nearby branch of the Shopi supermarket chain.

"What are you doing?" Lagrange said. "Where do you think you're going?"

"I'm going to buy some cognac," said Gloire.

"Excellent idea," approved Lagrange.

The best cognac at the Shopi cost 120 francs and 20 centimes in its stiff box; Gloire swung by the stationery aisle to get herself a roll of tape and another of striped, crinkled paper like seersucker. Back in the Opel, they headed off again; as they drove, she wrapped the box in the seersucker as best she could. It took a fair amount of time, but in the end, sure enough, it made a relatively presentable gift package. Lagrange had turned on the radio, which was playing J. J. Cale, of course, but also Boz Scaggs. Lagrange beat time with his index fingers on the wheel. He did not have the poor taste to ask for a sip of the cognac.

Rouen, then the suburbs of Rouen. Clusters of high-rises, a hospital, a cemetery, a retirement home; they parked in front of the retirement home. "Wait for me here," Gloire said, opening the car door. "I won't be long." Lagrange also had the tact not to suggest going in with her.

At the admissions desk, Gloire asked to see Mr. Abgrall. Kinship: only daughter. "Kindly wait a moment," they told her. At the end of that moment appeared a male nurse. A tall, handsome, young, immaculate type, very attentive, who seemed to know her father well, who spoke of him with affection, who brought Gloire to see him in ergotherapy.

In midconversation with a lady his age, Abgrall *père* stood up from his chair as they approached. Not tall, not fat, line of ashen mustache, looking lost but still elegant in his faded suit—an almost perfect double of Personnettaz's Slavic ex-concierge, but only we will ever know that—he kissed Gloire's hand as soon as it was within his reach. "It's your daughter, Mr. Abgrall," the nurse announced cheerfully. "You're glad to see her."

The old man studied Gloire intently, a hair too lengthily. "Very good," he said, "you've come for the distribution, that's good. You've come for the contribution. Please be seated." He turned to his contemporary: "She's come for the retribution," he confided to her in a half whisper.

Notwithstanding the peaceful activities of the old women all around them—crocheting, knitting, confection of artificial flowers and wicker baskets—a fair amount of noise reigned in the ergotherapy room. In their chairs of dirty plastic wire over rust-speckled tubing, toothless extroverts rocked dangerously while others sang in chorus ("Ah, the delight, the heady delight of the first time in his arms"). The smell was peculiar and the TV on full blast.

"Can't we find someplace a little quieter?" asked Gloire.

"Normally speaking, we can't," said the nurse, "but let me try to work something out for you. We'll find you a corner." The corner was a calm little room, dark at first glance, but the decidedly amenable nurse opened the curtains, revealing a clump of flowers on the lawn. The furniture was waxed, the wallpaper flowered, and the armchairs covered. The nurse disappeared, reappeared with tea, disappeared again. They were alone.

"So," said Gloire, "how are you?" "Personally, I'm fine," answered her father, "but it's the jays, you see." "What jays?" asked Gloire. "It's the jays who aren't doing so well," he specified. "One might even say they are not doing well at all. Well, actually," he amended after a moment's reflection, "they're not really doing so badly as all that." "Are you eating well?" his daughter inquired. "I'm eating better than they are," he winked. "Ten times better," he chuckled, "ten times more." "No," said Gloire, "I mean are they feeding you well? Is the food good?" "It's basically hot," answered her father. "Good," said Gloire, "it's better when it's hot." "That is correct," he said. "Did you see how beautiful it is outside?" she ventured, but her father seemed not to have heard this observation. "Here, I brought you this," she said again. "How very kind of you," he exclaimed, "what is it?" "It's some cognac for you," said Gloire, "you know, as usual." "Ah, cognac," he marveled. "I've never tried it." "Yeah, right," said Gloire, but the old man did not appear to register that comment either. "Well," she said, "I'm afraid I'd better be going." "That's true," he said dreamily, "sometimes one had better." "I'll come back and see you soon," she said. "Of course," he said, "you don't want to make yourself late."

After they had brought Abgrall senior back to ergotherapy, the nice male nurse escorted Gloire to the entrance. She rather liked that nurse. Before leaving, she asked him to keep an eye out that they didn't confiscate the cognac, as she was afraid they had done the previous time. "It's just that, normally speaking, alcoholic beverages aren't authorized either," the nurse smiled broadly, "but we always manage. I'll keep an eye out." Still, if there were to be a problem with the old gentleman, he worried, could Gloire leave a number where she could be reached, an address? She hesitated for a second—she really did like him —but no, she finally said; I'll call to check in.

Gloire left the retirement home and headed toward the Opel, parked on the gravel in front of a small administrative wing. A long ambulance with a sharklike white hood stood parked head-to-foot next to it. Gloire got into the Opel, which started up immediately, maneuvered, passed through the gateway, and disappeared. Five seconds later, the ambulance headed out in turn. On the porch of the retirement home, the nurse pondered this traffic. He stood immobile for five more seconds, then walked down the steps and went through the gateway in their wake. Fifty yards to the left, he entered a telephone booth and inserted into the apparatus a card decorated on the front with a snowy landscape, after absently gazing over the advertisement on the back: WITH THE PASSING OF THE SEASONS, OUTLOOKS AND FEELINGS CHANGE. YOU CAN SHARE THAT EMOTION WITH JUST THE TOUCH OF A BUTTON. This sentiment brought back his handsome smile, and then he punched in Jouve's number.

CHAPTER 25

"YOUR YOUNG WOMAN'S JUST BEEN HERE," the nurse announces. "Yes, she's already gone. No, no, she didn't leave an address, but I've got someone tailing her. I should know by tonight. I'll call you tomorrow. Now, about the money, how do we handle that?"

"We'll see tomorrow," answers Jouve before hanging up and turning toward his wife. "He can be pretty straight sometimes, that brother of yours. His tip worked out pretty well. Maybe we could have him over for dinner, what do you think?"

"Not on your life," answers Genevieve.

"Fine," says Jouve, "well, in the meantime I'll notify Personnettaz."

The next day flashed by at top speed. First Personnettaz showed up at around nine o'clock at the Jouves', who had just finished breakfast. Mrs. Jouve seemed less dazed, less nervous, more relaxed than usual. "You didn't bring the young lady from the other day?" she asked while pouring him the last of the coffee. Personnettaz pursed his lips instead of answering. "She's awfully pretty, you know," smiled Genevieve Jouve. "You're very lucky." Personnettaz tried to compose a detached face, managed only to turn purple and spill a quarter of his coffee into the saucer. Mrs. Jouve batted her eyelashes at this spectacle. Luckily for Personnettaz, the nice male nurse phoned back just then. He gave Gloire's address; Jouve noted the address. Then he asked again about the money; Jouve promised the money.

"So what should I do now?" asked Personnettaz.

"First you check with the client," said Jouve. "Don't forget to tell him about the little supplement for the nurse."

"That's not part of my functions," Personnettaz objected. "I'm happy to bring them up to date, but anything to do with money is your domain."

"Fine," agreed Jouve. "In any case, you should leave as soon as possible. Are you going alone?"

"I don't know yet," said Personnettaz, making sure not to meet the melting gaze of Mrs. Jouve. "I suppose. I don't know."

At ten twenty-five, Personnettaz left the Jouves and went to the head office of Stochastic, where, as of nine thirty, on the question of tall blonde women, Salvador had decided to change methodology. To take it all from scratch. To proceed in order. And first of all, what is it we call blondness? The French encyclopedias, which united in defining it as the median color between light brown and golden, mentioned no more than two or three shades: Venetian, ash, whatever. The Americans established a finer typology, distinguishing sandy blonde from copper blonde and platinum blonde from honey blonde, not to mention dirty blonde. And others besides. Good. Onward.

But at five past eleven, Personnettaz arrived to interrupt Salvador's reflections. Salvador was there alone; Donatienne hadn't shown up yet. "It's done," Personnettaz informed him, "they've found her. This time it's for real."

"Well, go on then," Salvador said distractedly, "go on then."

"I'm afraid it just won't be that easy," Personnettaz objected. "You've seen how difficult she can be."

"This really is too much," remarked Salvador. "Why is she so wild? We don't mean the girl any harm. Why does she act like that?"

"That," said Personnettaz, "I don't know."

But he does know, or at least he has his little theory. Salvador and his assistant seem to be taken aback by Gloire's behavior, find the harshness of her reactions quite out of proportion to the guilelessness of their project. Personnettaz somehow finds it all understandable. He isn't convinced that dragging someone onto a TV screen is such an innocent maneuver. Still, he lets none of this show.

"Well," suggests Salvador, "take Donatienne with you if you're worried, ask her to go along. It's better if there are two of you."

"Yes," says Personnettaz, "perhaps." He hesitates. He does not like hesitating. Not only does he always have trouble with Donatienne, but she also occupies much too much of his mental space.

And here she is, arriving at around eleven thirty; they fill her in on the situation. "So," she says, "are we going?"

"Well, I mean," Personnettaz hears himself answering, "well, yes. Let's go." They converse for a few minutes more, then head off a little before twelve in Donatienne's car.

But between the heavy traffic on the highway and the time to grab a quick bite en route, then to find their way from the nurse's directions, it was easily three o'clock before they located the manor. They parked the vehicle at the junction of two low walls, affording a discreetly impregnable view of the entrance to the property. When Donatienne pulled a pack of cigarettes out of her bag, Personnettaz lowered the window on his side by a third.

Luck was with them: they didn't have to wait long. After no more than an hour, Gloire appeared alone at the wheel of Lagrange's Opel. They recognized her, followed her at a distance as she turned onto the road for Honfleur. Personnettaz drove very delicately, manipulating the gear shift and steering wheel with the tips of his fingers, avoiding the slightest mechanical creaking as if any sudden movement might compromise the situation—in short, rolling on eggshells. "Really," he thought to himself, "we've traveled to the other end of the world to find her, we've missed her every time, and now here she is, a few yards away."

The weather was still beautiful, almost as beautiful as the day before: at five past four, Gloire sat at an outside table of a bar on the port and ordered a beer. It seemed as if she might have been expecting something or someone. Sitting at a contiguous terrace, Donatienne who was drinking an orangeade and Personnettaz a club soda did not let her out of the edge of their sight. They were pretending to have a conversation, like extras in the movies supposedly talking to each other in the background, inaudible: their lips moved in the void and their dialogues were made of mush. In any case, Personnettaz always had trouble talking calmly with Donatienne, and this fact filled him with suffering and resentment.

Not only did he not know how to talk to Donatienne, but he wasn't sure how to proceed with Gloire either. He was still hesitating. Indeed, what to do? Talk to her. Convince her that they meant her no harm. Make off with her by force. Or by gentle persuasion. Experience had pretty much shown that any surveillance, any attempt to approach or contact her would meet with a violent response. They would see; they would try to do their best.

Gloire stood up at twenty-five to five. They had to follow her on foot. She headed toward the modest, chalky light-house that stood not far from the port, toward Trouville, on a small overhang bordering a cliff of modest dimensions. It should be mentioned that Gloire—who had already noticed, the evening before, that a wheezy ambulance without revolving lights had been following them since Rouen—had naturally spotted the unidentified convertible that began tailing her anew near Honfleur. She acted as if nothing were the matter.

At five minutes to five, Gloire will push open the small door at the base of the lighthouse—no smaller than any other door, actually, but looking crushed by virtue of an optical illusion—and close it behind her. In the eyes of her persecutors, this lighthouse is the perfect trap in which to catch her at last: with Donatienne behind him, Personnettaz will enter it in turn. He will climb the 120 spiraling stairs. He will step out into the open air, onto the narrow circular platform above the port. He will have time to notice the more or less parallel waves, coming to beat gently on the shore like written lines breaking against a margin. Nervous gusts of wind, passage of seagulls in an atmosphere that is sharper than on ground level, retracted sunlight too cold to be blinding. Donatienne will appear several seconds later. So it is at five o'clock sharp that Gloire, surging from a slight recess, will surprise Personnettaz from behind and, as she knows how to do so well, forcefully knock him over the guardrail. We've already said that it isn't a large lighthouse, almost a toy, a prop for a low-budget film. Falling from it would not necessarily kill you. But if you were lucky enough to survive, you could still get seriously hurt and would never be the same.

Everything happened exactly as we have just predicted, except that at the very last moment—5:00:03—as

Personnettaz was tipping over into the void, Beliard decided to intervene. He who never appeared in the visible social order had just resolved to publicly display his superpowers. Appearing out of nowhere, Beliard hurled himself toward Donatienne, grabbed her by the waist, and sent her flying in turn toward Personnettaz. The young woman didn't have time to be afraid. As parachutists waltz in free fall in midsky, she joined Personnettaz in the air, gripped him solidly by the shoulders, and led him, still remote-controlled by the homunculus, back to the lighthouse platform. All of it very fast, over in just a few seconds; no one understood a thing—just as after an epileptic seizure, when no one really wants to understand what has just happened. Personnettaz, eyes wild, straightened his clothes; then, getting ahold of himself, made his introduction: Jean-Charles Personnettaz, pleased to meet you. "Gloire Abgrall," said Gloire. They stared at each other without affection but without hostility; everyone seemed very tired. No one saw Beliard quietly slip away, brushing his hands against each other and puffing out his chest, smoothing back his hair on both sides, and that takes care of that.

CHAPTER 26

"WE DON'T MEAN YOU ANY HARM," said Personnettaz. "I don't, in any case. What will you have?"

They had left the lighthouse for the port. Day was waning. Gently it waned in nautilus pink, a pink of gladiolas and strawberries with cream. It had now gotten too chilly to colonize another outdoor table; they had immersed themselves in the seats of the Hôtel de l'Absinthe bar. At that hour the clientele was sparse. A bartender wiped off the pedestal table, awaited their order, looked like George Sanders.

"Dry martini," said Gloire.

"Good idea," said Donatienne. "Yes, dry martini."

"Right, so three dry martinis," Personnettaz said to George, showing three fingers.

As a rule, Personnettaz avoids alcohol, but after the lighthouse incident everyone needed a pick-me-up. They were slightly dazed, as if after a match or opening night, when one recovers from one's efforts in the locker or dressing room. One has left behind one's role, one's trunks, one's costume. One redons civilian garb, returns to real life. One catches one's breath. One might exchange peaceable, considerate, muffled statements, but for those first few minutes one says absolutely nothing.

As a rule, Personnettaz also avoids tobacco; but feeling a rare urge, he got up for a moment. When he returned, packing ultralights equipped with three-tiered filters, Donatienne had begun explaining their mission. Detailing her job in television production, her work methods, her plans for broadcasts—among which the one that they hoped to do on Gloire, the reason they had been chasing after her for two months. They were still quite set on it, on that broadcast; Donatienne was very set on it, as was her boss, named Salvador. Would Gloire agree, now, to be part of it? Gloire, without answering, opened her eyes wide.

Donatienne assured her that people still remembered her, that they would be very interested to know what had become of her; Gloire was anything but certain she wanted them to know. "I'm not really sure," she said. "I'll have to think about it."

"Anyway, we won't do anything without your OK," said Donatienne, "never fear. All I ask is that you meet Salvador. After that you can do as you like."

Besides, don't forget that the pay wouldn't be so bad either, you see. They were not short on cash. They had already spent a bundle searching for Gloire at the other end of the world—at these words, Personnettaz lit a cigarette. As Donatienne rapidly summarized this search, no mention was made of its violent episodes. No allusion, for example, to Jean-Claude Kastner, nor to the lighthouse episode from an hour before.

That visit to the lighthouse, furthermore, seemed to have been forgotten by Personnettaz and Donatienne. Unless they preferred not to mention it, not being entirely sure of its reality—one does not mention one's hallucinations, which pertain strictly to one's private life. As far as Gloire was concerned, she was not too keen on having strangers become interested in Beliard, in his little excursions into reality. Moreover, she always distrusted reality somewhat when Beliard deigned to get involved in it. Personnettaz lit a second cigarette, of which, as with the first, he inhaled almost nothing, given the density of the filter.

Donatienne did her best to convince Gloire of the soundness of her offer. Money, fame, success regained, why not the beginning of a new career, and even love while we're at it, and shall we order another round? They had another round, then Gloire stood up to take her leave. "If you want to talk it over some more," said Donatienne, "meet me here tomorrow, late morning. Take tonight to decide, think it over."

Violins erupt at Gloire's departure. First an attack in the minor key when she abruptly stands; then a vertiginous bass whirl when she throws a last look at Donatienne and Personnettaz; finally a series of brief staccato attacks as she moves off toward the cylindrical revolving doors of the entrance. Personnettaz finds himself alone with Donatienne.

"I wouldn't mind one for the road," says Donatienne. "I know it's not the sensible thing, but what the hell, now that we've gotten that over with—how about you?"

"No," says Personnettaz, "I'm fine as is."

Nervously he rips the filter off a third cigarette before reducing it to ash with a single draw. Then he hesitates, not very sure of himself.

"Did you notice anything before, on the lighthouse?"

"Uh, no," says Donatienne. "Why?"

"No," says Personnettaz, "nothing."

Personnettaz, even if he's not sure, nonetheless believes he remembers seeing Donatienne, a little while before, flying through the air to save him from probable death. But he prefers not to insist. "So, we're not going back tonight?" he segues.

"It's late," opines Donatienne. "Aren't you tired? And besides, we might have to see the girl again tomorrow. They must have rooms here. It seems nice, this hotel."

They did in fact have rooms available, and they were in fact nice. Deluxe category as in Bombay, but silkier, more intimate, and with a view of the Channel instead of the Gulf of Oman. Their windows overlooked it from two different floors. They would rest in their rooms for an hour, then would meet for dinner. Personnettaz watched Donatienne walk away toward the elevator.

When he took it in turn, the cabin was better lit than at the Cosmopolitan Club but, under the vertical spotlight near the back mirror, Personnettaz saw himself aging just the same. From the bottom of his heart he never would have thought such a thing could happen to him, ever. Hadn't even imagined it. Proceeding as if it were impossible, as if none of this concerned him, as if he weren't even there, he must have vaguely counted on time forgetting all about him. But time caught up with him from behind, growing ever-larger in the rearview mirror and preparing to overtake him. Personnettaz brushed away this idea. It was just that he had to get ready; it was just that, with Donatienne, he would have to keep himself in check all through dinner.

Personnettaz entered his room and lay down while awaiting the dinner hour. He intended to think awhile on his bed, but he fell asleep, briefly dreamed, then awoke with a start just in time. Feeling some apprehension, he inspected his face in the bathroom mirror before going back downstairs. Less offensive than the one in the elevator, this mirror was still not well disposed toward its user, the proof being that Personnettaz spotted a pimple on the left wing of his nose.

In theory, popping a pimple is no big deal, a matter of a lit-tle alcohol on cotton. Having no ninety-percent alcohol in his shaving kit, Personnettaz searched feverishly in the mini-bar for some liquid to take its place. Rather than amber spirits, such as cognac or whiskey, a transparent alcohol approximating the pharmaceutical kind would no doubt do the trick better: gin, aquavit, vodka. Probably vodka, all things considered, with which Personnettaz imbibed a kleenex and dabbed himself—after which, to bolster his courage, he swallowed the remaining contents of the minia-ture bottle in one gulp. Which wasn't like him. Already the cigarettes, a short while ago, weren't like him. None of this was normal behavior. Personnettaz didn't recognize himself.

Gloire, meanwhile, had gone off in Lagrange's car; on the road she soliloquized. The Opel's headlights conically perforated the fallen night, projecting the film of the day's events on the twin curtain of poplars. Gloire had barely reacted to Donatienne's proposals, neither accepting nor refusing, saying nothing. She found her rather likable, that girl, fairly attractive in a curvy energetic brunette sort of way. She was undecided. Returning to the manor at around nine o'clock, she ran into Lagrange in the foyer. The half-drunk Lagrange claimed to have been worried, complained that he had waited for her for dinner. "Did you see what time it is," he went, poking his index finger at his wrist, before jerk-ing his erect thumb at the kitchen. "It's all cold now."

"Just give me two more minutes," said Gloire. "I'm coming."

Having vanished from the lighthouse immediately after his lightning intervention, Beliard must have returned to her room. Before anything else, she wanted to consult him.

"So," exclaimed the homunculus as soon as Gloire had opened the door, "was I good or what?"

He seemed content with the afternoon's exploit. Had they talked about it, he wanted to know. "No," answered Gloire, "they didn't say a word."

"Typical," Beliard clouded over. "Still, I wouldn't mind somebody noticing once in a while. Sometimes you need a little public support."

"Yeah," she said, "I don't know. Don't you think we would have been better off getting rid of them?"

Resting a finger on his temple, Beliard explained that he'd considered it, but that he didn't believe so. First of all, he wouldn't have saved Personnettaz if he'd thought him dangerous. And more generally, he deemed that it was time for Gloire to go back to legal methods, to return to human society. It was all right for Jean-Claude Kastner, even for the guy in Sydney, but they couldn't very well keep on giving intruders the shove forever. Despite all his powers, despite his invisibility, one day or another someone would end up noticing. Wouldn't it be better to come to terms now, try to bow to the common order? It might be a little difficult at first, after years spent living on the edge, but he, Beliard, would be there to help her. So what did that girl want, anyway? Grudgingly, Gloire told him of Donatienne's cathodic proposal. "Perfect," said Beliard, "couldn't ask for better timing. It's the chance of a lifetime."

"You really think so?" murmured Gloire.

"Of course," said Beliard. "Let's go for it. You won't get another shot like this. Go eat something, now. You'll need to be in shape for tomorrow."

Gloire went down to join Lagrange, sitting alone in front of the glasses in the dining room. While they ate their cold dinner, his eyelids drooped several times. He didn't seem to register the announcement of Gloire's departure, found in it only a pretext to pour himself another one. Gloire left the table before he did.

Lagrange was still asleep the next morning when Gloire phoned the Hôtel de l'Absinthe; Personnettaz and Donatienne appeared an hour later. Gloire's bags hopped by themselves into the trunk of the convertible that shortly afterward headed down the western highway. Personnettaz and Donatienne sat in front, while Gloire, sitting to the right, behind them, stared at the road framed by their asymmetrical shoulders; the traffic flowed under a milky sky. After agreeing that they would bring her straight to see Salvador the moment they arrived in Paris, they didn't say much more to each other. Personnettaz turned the pages of a magazine and only once did Gloire's eyes meet Donatienne's in the rearview mirror. "We haven't even discussed money," the latter nonetheless said near Mantes-la-Jolie. "Would two hundred thousand do?" (As Gloire takes her time answering, Beliard appears fleetingly on the seat beside her. Quick wink and rapid smile: he stretches out four fingers and waves them.) "Four hundred thousand," said Gloire. "Four hundred thousand it is," said Donatienne. (Beliard nods, smiles more widely, and gives a thumbs up before evaporating.) They were almost there.

Southern beltway: eight or nine exits separated Auteuil from Porte Dorée, where Gloire got out. Donatienne, who would come back to pick her up a little later, mentioned that they'd reserved a room for her in a hotel near the Mosque. They headed off.

"Where to now?" asked Personnettaz.

"We could always go get a drink somewhere," suggested Donatienne, "or else I can give you a lift where you're going."

It seemed to Personnettaz that he reflected for a long time before hearing himself propose to the young woman that that drink, while they were at it, could just as well be had at his place.

"Why not," she said against all hope, "if you'd rather. Which way?"

"Head toward République," said Personnettaz in a blank voice. "I live right next to it."

All along the boulevards his heart was in his shoes, particularly since it was always difficult to park in his neighborhood. By a lucky break, a spot had just come free in his street, just opposite his building. He tried to think of something to say about that lucky break, about the street, about life; one of those elevated, witty, well-observed pronouncements that beautify existence: but no, nothing for the moment. Or yes, actually, perhaps—but as he was about to open his mouth, someone tapped unpleasantly on the window next to him. Personnettaz turned around: Boccara was grinning broadly at him and making signs on the other side of the glass, notably the sign to lower it. Personnettaz lowered the window.

"What are you doing here?" he asked.

"What a stroke of luck!" Boccara enthused. "I wanted to see you and *voilà*, here you are!"

Back from his cruise, he was appreciably tanned, wearing a new suit that was a bit too yellow and light for the season; he had gained a few pounds. Donatienne looked at him. Personnettaz was embarrassed.

"So just like that," he went, "you're back."

"I had a great time," said Boccara, "and man, you won't believe some of the things I've seen. I'm kind of sorry it's over. I met some girls like you wouldn't believe. I came over to tell you all about it."

"Listen—" Personnettaz began.

"Well," Donatienne interrupted him, grasping the gearshift, "I'll leave you with your friend."

"Hang on," said Personnettaz, then, turning toward her: "Wait, that drink," he whispered, "I thought we'd said—"

"Another time," smiled Donatienne. "You can call me if you feel like it."

"But—" repeated Personnettaz.

She continued to smile as she shifted into first, made a sign with her head before moving off, and was gone. The smile lingered, intact, up to the end of Rue Yves-Toudic; then it would play some more about her lips for the entire length of Boulevard Magenta.

"What's the matter?" said Boccara. "You don't look so good."

"Nothing," said Personnattaz, watching the convertible disappear. "Nothing."

If he is naturally a little annoyed at Boccara, a rival sentiment of slight relief keeps him from holding too much of a grudge against the young man—who is also watching Donatienne vanish into the distance. That's how it is: left to themselves, they watch her go.

"Boy," said Boccara, "she's really stacked."

"Oh, really," Personnettaz said noncommittally while searching his pockets. "You think so?"

"How well do you know her?" worried Boccara.

"A little," Personnettaz answered modestly, pulling out his cigarettes. "I know her a little."

"You son of a gun," said Boccara.

CHAPTER 27

"THE SUN," SALVADOR SAYS TO HIMSELF.

He has been seeking new ideas for his project since early morning, without coming up with a single one, as usual. The sky is very overcast; sporadically it rains on Porte Dorée. Salvador is not happy. Whether his mood derives from his mental sterility, the rotten weather, or this wasted time is hard to say. But around noon it begins to clear and the clouds break up. Through the windows the sunlight throws out large bright parallelograms onto the floor, casts trapezoids into the corners with ricochets of reflections. If dazzling weather still does not flood his soul, at least Salvador thinks: the sun.

Let us, he proposes to himself, look into the effects of the sun's rays on tall blondes. Let us ponder. No half measures with it: the sun bronzes you or burns you, it colors or kills. If it generously tans the warm, triumphant tall blondes, it pitilessly carbonizes the refrigerated, chlorotic ones. Too porous and translucent, the chlorotic tall blondes immediately redden, heat up, and shrivel away. Only the triumphant ones remain, the ones whose portrait we tried to sketch in Chapter Eleven. Their denser epidermis, their more resistant complexion give the ultraviolets a hero's welcome. Yes, Salvador says to himself, let us examine, let us turn our attention to the tanned tall blondes. At that moment the door opens, and lo and behold a tanned tall blonde appears.

Feminine, masculine, neuter: if the sun's gender varies from one language to another, its character also changes depending on the skies. And the fact is that, subjected to the abrupt Australian sun, then to the more enveloping rays of the Indian one, Gloire has browned quite a bit since her departure. Salvador hesitates. For a moment he understands nothing—as if his idea has just been made flesh by magic before his eyes—then he identifies the young woman. Such encounters might provoke a short-circuit, an indraft followed by a blaze; they might unleash fireworks in the heart of a rainbow, accompanied by another cascade of the string orchestra. And that's exactly what happens in the resuscitated spirit of Salvador, who suddenly appears extremely self-conscious. Yes, it's his body that doesn't seem to be in synch: "Oh, right," he lurches up crookedly, "right. Come in."

He bangs against his desk as he comes around to meet Gloire, stops too far from, then too close to, her, can't decide whether to put out his hand, which he finally waves vaguely at an armchair. In the time it takes for him to regain his seat and for Gloire to identify the armchair, we hear quite a number of cars pass by on Avenue du Général-Dodds.

"I was expecting you," Salvador claims.

But he talks to her as if reluctantly, and twenty minutes later Gloire still doesn't know much more than she did the day before from Donatienne. Salvador, meanwhile, is no more relaxed than before. He has given Gloire every possible detail: shooting in late May, travel, commentary, archival documents, film clips, four days in the studio, editing, mixing, broadcast in late September; he has attempted parenthetical clauses, ventured generalities, but without even daring to offer her a drink. So. He wanted her consent, she has granted it, so now what? There remain only silences, averted gazes, composure lost without a trace; the whole thing begins to drag on, and Salvador is abominably perturbed. Fortunately, Donatienne shows up right on time to cut this conversation short. Gloire tries not to appear too relieved. "So, well, then, goodbye," Salvador says awkwardly. "So see you soon, I guess."

Afterward, beneath the reemerging sun, Gloire and Donatienne slice the twelfth arrondissement down the middle, cross the Seine via the Pont d'Austerlitz, then skirt the Jardin des Plantes toward the Mosque. If men talk about women, in cars and elsewhere, we now know that the reverse is also true: as they drive through Paris, the two women swap opinions of Personnettaz—whom they both find somewhat peculiar—then of Salvador, who Donatienne confirms is also a bit peculiar.

Peculiar or not, he tries to get back to work after their departure, but it's no good, he's too distracted. Salvador paces around his office, looks out the window, tries to read a few pages of *How to Disappear Completely and Never Be Found* without managing to get absorbed in it. Shuts the book, which he throws into a plastic bag; folds his notes in four and slips them into his pocket; then gets up from his chair. Decides to go home. Leaves. Walks down into the Metro. Absentmindedly waits for the train without really waiting. It comes; he gets on. Standing, back against the doors of the subway car, once he has cast an empty glance at his neighbors—resigned old people, hirsute readers of computer magazines, a Senegalese girl with ice skates—he pulls the book from his bag. But since the bag keeps him from holding the bag comfortably, he tries to get rid of it by putting the book in the bag, but no, since it's the same bag—shit. No two ways about it, he's rather distracted.

Back home, in his half kitchen, after some leftovers and the evening news, Salvador unfolds, rereads, absently develops his notes; forces himself to banish Gloire from his mind. Let's start again. So, the triumphant tall blondes welcome the sun, absorb it, assimilate it, then wear it. In the form of pigments. Thus, on summer evenings, in nightclubs, crossing their endless legs on high stools, they shine like portable suns. The sun, concludes Salvador, is itself a tall blonde.

At that same moment, on Rue Yves-Toudic, Personnettaz is also sitting in his small kitchen, but he has come to different conclusions while puffing on cigarettes. It seems that since yesterday Personnettaz has taken up smoking again. Two empty glasses are on the table before him: recounting his adventures made Boccara thirsty, while drinking made him talkative. At that point, it could have gone on forever, and Personnettaz had begun to worry he might never leave. Boccara has said goodbye only a short while ago. In any case, Personnettaz didn't listen to his whole story, preferring to recall the young man's appraisal of Donatienne, pronounced that very afternoon. After the unabridged narrative of his cruise, Personnettaz had to cut in the moment Boccara threatened to segue into his love life. Personnettaz is finally alone.

He is alone but he is agitated. It's just that feelings are not his strong point. Up until now, for him, love has always appeared without witnesses. Each time it has occurred, Personnettaz, not very secure in his judgments or his emotions, has hastened to bring it to an end. With no outside opinion, he has given up. But let a witness happen to encourage him—the other day Mrs. Jouve, today Boccara—

and anything seems possible. Love, as we know, often passes via third parties, whoever they are and whatever they say. Order or advice, permission or prescription, no matter: the main thing is that it pushes you onward. This said, Personnettaz bitterly admits that it's a pretty unlikely match. There's still the fact that Donatienne is much more beautiful (I mean more beautiful that I am handsome), no doubt much better off financially (which isn't hard), and significantly younger (see above).

In short, things have drifted to such a point in our tale that we now have two men who are smitten with two distinctly different women. What will happen? How will this all turn out?

CHAPTER 28

SIX MONTHS LATER, during the broadcast of the program devoted to Gloire, Personnettaz seduced Donatienne or vice versa. That Thursday evening he wasn't expecting anything in particular when she appeared unannounced at his door, claiming her TV was on the fritz. She made no comments about Personnettaz's apartment: nearly empty, it didn't lend itself to any. With regard to the only decorative object, a green plant on its last legs, Donatienne merely gave some resuscitation advice. Personnettaz had nothing to offer her but some dregs of kirsch that they split but did not touch. When showtime came, Personnettaz turned on his set, offered Donatienne the only chair he owned, and took his place next to her on an old stool. Then, even if we don't know exactly what phrases, what glances were exchanged, which of those two pieces of furniture first moved toward the other before Personnettaz and Donatienne stretched out on a third, one thing at least is certain: they didn't watch the show to the end.

The following Sunday, Personnettaz moved into Donatienne's, renouncing in a single gesture and with no

regrets his little home on Rue Yves-Toudic and his intermittent chores for Jouve. His diet immediately improved,
his wardrobe was renewed, his face relaxed a bit—in short,
his life was transformed. He even began to cultivate the
idea of one fine day marrying that beautiful woman, even
if Donatienne Personnettaz might be a bit of a mouthful,
as names go.

Since one door closes and another one opens, Jouve,
faced with this defection, had to resign himself to replacing Personnettaz with Boccara as his first agent. In keeping
with that promotion, the latter deemed it necessary that
they immediately recruit an assistant. Three days later,
Jouve found him a new operative answering to the name
of Patrick Berthomieux. Patrick Berthomieux was a pensive,
reserved, frail boy who in all seasons wore a supernumer-
ary sweater. He was always fearful of bothering people,
Patrick Berthomieux—a major drawback when one prac-
ticed his profession. He was barely younger than Boccara,
who, nostalgic for Personnettaz, saw no better means of hon-
oring the latter's memory than to behave with Berthomieux
as the other had acted with him.

Nor, the day after his promotion, on the occasion of a
visit to Jouve who was, as usual, out, did Boccara find any
better project than to seduce Genevieve Jouve. It occurred
to him two days later that this prospect was a dead end,
not such a good idea after all. As early as the following weekend, staking out with Patrick Berthomieux the home of an
engineer suspected by his firm, Boccara confided his recent
woes to his assistant. As he had been used to doing with
Personnettaz, he ruminated aloud: "You see, Patrick," he
explained, "love is a lot like snow in Paris. It's very pretty
when it falls on you, but it doesn't stay that way. And afterward it gets all fucked up. It either turns to ice or to slush,
but very soon it becomes more trouble than it's worth."

"Really, Gilbert?" answered Berthomieux. "Do you think so?"

"Yes," said Boccara, "I do think so. But I especially think, and please don't forget it, that it's 'Mr. Boccara' to you."

"Oh, right," Berthomieux caught himself. "Sorry, Mr. Boccara."

Broadcast in prime time, with an average of 16.2 points and a 35.6 percent market share, Salvador's series was a huge success. It was watched in many homes. Genevieve Jouve didn't miss a minute of it on her sofa, nor did Lagrange and Zbigniew in their prison cell at Fresnes. In one stroke, Stochastic Films solidified its positions with the hertzian channels and Salvador had his contract renewed. Given those conditions, he had no trouble negotiating a few weeks away in the mountains, in order to put the finishing touches on a few other projects. Then he packed his bags.

As another consequence of that broadcast, Gloire had to bear the burdens of her new popularity. People once again recognized her in the street, sent her sacks of mail, offered her spots in TV commercials or nude poses in certain magazines, and even the chance to remix her old hits. But we know all too well how fragile she is. After having enjoyed the situation for fifteen minutes, she quickly went back to hiding out, stopped eating, stopped opening her door or answering the telephone. Gloire's behavior ended up worrying the staff of the hotel behind the Mosque, which she hadn't left. Immediately notified, and although quite preoccupied by her new life with Personnettaz, Donatienne flew to her side, became alarmed, and did her best to pacify Gloire before letting Salvador know.

Impressing upon him the fact that he was responsible for the young woman's state, Donatienne ended up convincing Salvador to look after her, take care of her, protect her from others and from herself. At first, Salvador couldn't hide his reticence: this wasn't at all what he had in mind. Deeply impressed by Gloire but burned by life, he would much rather practice prevention than risk needing a cure. Lowering an iron curtain over his feelings, he had scrupulously kept his distance from the young woman during the shooting. But enjoined by Donatienne, he finally yielded. He took the situation in hand.

Before buckling his suitcase, then, he made sure that another room was available in the hotel where he had his reservation: a small, comfortable inn run by two sisters in a ski resort in the Pyrenees. Salvador was known there. "No problem," the older sister answered. "Not many people this early in the season." They left in the car.

They arrived at the end of the day. Gloire's room was furnished in white wood. Sun and detergents had bleached the curtains and the quilt; the sheets were just slightly starched. Through the window, in the distance, she saw two sharp, rocky protuberances standing out in the twilight, scanning the horizon like an encephalogram: the base of one was linked by a funicular to the crest of the other. After dinner, worn out from the trip, she went up to bed early, vaguely counting on a visit from Beliard without really wanting it. But not tonight. Tonight, no one.

The fact is, Beliard was seen less and less often. Since the broadcast of *Tall Blondes,* his interventions had become scarce. And, less regular than ever, in those moments when he did appear it was like a whirlwind. Soon Gloire caught only fleeting glimpses of him, looking rushed like a businessman between two trains, wearing a new suit, checking his watch every five minutes, as well as a little appointment book that she'd never seen before. Nonchalantly, Beliard started hinting at some new contacts.

The day after their arrival, Salvador suggested they go for a walk, counting on the mountain air to restore the young woman's equilibrium. At that altitude and in that season, if the air proved to be a bit chilly at night, in the afternoon it nonetheless donned its summer garb again. Gloire and Salvador walked, not speaking much, not always side by side, as if they barely knew each other. Their exchanges were stamped with the distant courtesy systematically adopted by warring shipwreck survivors forced to share the same desert island. Salvador, who knew the area, occasionally specified the name of a flower they came across, the name of a passing bird; they left it at that. Gloire would have plenty of time later on to look up those names in her little English nature guides.

For a first day, they walked pretty far. Their steps brought them to one of the two sharp protuberances that Gloire could see from her window. They reached the base of it, from which one could take the funicular to the crest of the other. They were dressed in light-colored clothes, and the weather was almost hot. Gloire went ahead first; Salvador followed a few yards behind, jacket flung over his shoulder. Under the pylon, near a small wooden hut—a simple kiosk with penthouse roof and a ticket window— the empty cabin of the funicular looked like an old-model tram in the station or a docked ferry boat. The torso of a man with sun-baked face and thick fingers, dressed in an anorak, emerged from the window frame beside a fat roll of tickets. The surroundings were silent; not a living soul as far as the eye could see, except for Salvador, Gloire, and that man, who also sold postcards of the landscape.

After consulting the posted fees, Gloire buys two tickets just as Salvador joins her. The man inside the kiosk gets up to go activate the launch mechanism. "Wait a minute," says Salvador, "hold on there. I can't get in that thing." Gloire gives him a quizzical look. "I'm a bit sensitive about heights," explains Salvador. "I can't stand to have them under me. It makes me feel ill, if you see what I mean. I'm afraid of them. It's absurd, but there's nothing I can do about it."

Gloire stares at him with a funny, slightly frozen smile. Her eyes are almost liquid. "Come on, come with me," she says in a strange voice. And Salvador, as if devoid of will, follows her toward the cabin. The door shuts behind them as soon as the man outside his kiosk has manipulated handles and levers, then pushed a big green button: the funicular gives a silent lurch, and they lift off. It climbs away. Standing near the machines, the man watches the cabin shrink, while above it eagles, or perhaps vultures, describe new circles in the open sky. A very light wind plays a few intermittent harmonics on the cables of the funicular—whose cabin, halfway up, comes to a sudden halt. Still no sign of Beliard.

You're expecting the worst, and that's understandable. Scared to death, unable to risk the slightest downward glance, Salvador clings with all his might to whatever looks like a handle, squeezes it so tightly that his joints turn white, that he can't breathe. But Gloire is there, smiling at him, moving close and placing two fingers on his shoulder while whispering for him not to be afraid. Her hand comes sliding from Salvador's shoulder to his neck, then to the back of his neck; Salvador's hair is divided between her fingers. And then the next moment, letting go of all his handles, it's the young woman that he squeezes in his arms.

While she is against him, his lips on her neck, Salvador opens one eye and, over Gloire's shoulder, distinctly sees the abyss. Now, miracle number one, no vertigo seizes him, no dizziness; all his cardinal points remain in place, in peaceful harmony with the dimensions. And Gloire, miracle number two, does not at all envision letting this man fall into the void, nor even perhaps letting him fall out of her life in the future. Quite possibly she'll never need Beliard again (assuming he wasn't responsible for these developments to begin with), for between heaven and earth Salvador and Gloire are still kissing. And begin over and over. And do not seem to want to stop. To see their faces this way, their bodies, it appears that neither of them is feeling any pain at the moment, any particular worry. He is no longer afraid of the void. She is no longer afraid of anything.